Bottled Cries at Sea

Bottled Cries at Sea

Stories by Jean E. Verthein

atmosphere press

© 2021 Jean E. Verthein

Published by Atmosphere Press

Cover design by Nick Courtright

No part of this book may be reproduced without permission from the author except in brief quotations and in reviews. This is a work of fiction, and any resemblance to real places, persons, or events is entirely coincidental.

atmospherepress.com

Contents

For the Sake of Artie

Fat Man exploded, leveling buildings and hanging over the city. Missing this reckoning, the first foreign merchant ship near there, Artie's, began sweeping into the port of Nagasaki.

In this harbor of the Pacific, while the ship was buoying, he, a crewman, was leaning on its railing. At its prow, waves of the sea were entrancing and vexing him. Fluctuating like features: eyes, their sockets, noses, mouths, and chins rose and fell. They shaped and joined into masks, separated, and dissolved.

* * *

After the war and its last summer in 1945, the city he never forgot became "Kumoi in Nagasaki." Artie reflected on her with his kid brother, anticipating joy. Up to then, he'd lived a knockabout life. Without consent for his first trip out, he'd bolted from home in the Village to the old Market Street pier on New York's Lower East Side. At his first ship in the Caribbean, no one bothered to check his age at 15, though anyone could spot him: six feet five, 140 pounds, blue eyes, and sand crew cut. He signed onto a ship that was bound to and back from ports, such as Miami, Ponce, Port-au-Prince, Salvador, San Felipe, Corinto.

There, he and other mariners would unload their

ship, and then lay about for days or months. For play, he could choose between bethels without women or brothels or bars with prossies.

“Every guy on my ship," he told his kid brother back in New York, "ran into the cat house." Tall enough to peer in, he could see inside, but he was too skinny to buck the two big guys holding him down. "The whole damn shipload of 'em got stung with clap there. I was the only one on ship who didn’t catch it or, worse, have to deal with the cure.”

Back home, his voyage out failed to impress his pop, who grabbed him on the dock. All the way home, he chewed Artie out about the dangers of shore-to-ship life and warned him about getting roped into going every which way.

His pop threw him back into the high school he hated. “I got through it by reading every book in sight and never knocking a girl up. No mother’d let one near a mariner, but I was the most virginal kid in my class, and the smartest.”

* * *

When Tojo ordered the bombing and torpedoing in 1941 of Pearl Harbor in Hawaii, Artie was still in high school. The too-young son and his too-old father leaped toward the war effort. Only the Merchant Marine would take them from the Port of New York.

Not far offshore, warring ships or submarines were sinking each other under the Atlantic, and enemy seamen, some said, were swimming to shore. Local people stood watch along Coney Island and Sheepshead

Bay. This biggest merchant marine departure point for World War II launched the Arties with thousands more. Father and son embarked in separate ships.

On his first voyage across the Atlantic, his ship glided past Gibraltar on to Genoa. Artie's ship docked at Aqaba on the Red Sea. There he saw his first slave market. There, a giant presided. His brown pants billowed below his crimson cummerbund. Without auctioning off anyone, he sliced off the right hand of a robber that plopped and rolled. Its forefinger seemed pointed toward Artie.

"A dishonor to lose your right hand," an old Brit told Artie through his gray hedge beard in the café, where water bubbled in their water pipes, hookahs, and Artie saluted him and said, "Seamen like you get treated like scum."

"Not me." All the same, he toasted with tea in a glass cup, from which sunlight gleamed through like burnt sienna as Artie saw hand for a hand justice en route to bomb for a bomb.

* * *

Sailing farther East, near Calcutta, Artie chanced on bathers, preparing for death near charnel house workers sorting bleached bones. Charred and cracked cadaver debris they let spill down, whole bones that could be pieced together to create anatomy class skeletons.

Live folks resembled cinnamon sticks, and skeletal women crinkled in their glorious bright saris, loud in reds, greens, and yellows. Working, they were plucking usable goods from garbage. Others in pastels or white kurtas rode in carts, pulled by skinny muscled men. Watching this ever arousing and enthusing populace, its young and old perpetually asked, “What is your mission in India?” Artie checked his funny bone. “Go my way to the Far East."

Back on-board ship, Artie fused endless guesswork with off-hours of

reading donated books, pulps, encyclopedias, and histories to relieve the tedium that gnawed at him when ship-bound.

A guide revealed the way inland to Khajuraho on a range of blue-flowered greenery. While the train was rattling along, Artie crouched to jump with a buddy to stride across fields to behold the *nautch* dancers, bursting off the temple walls. Sculpted couplings amused him, like practice for his own flesh. Not far away, live Indian women bared their midriffs for him though screens, their bodies in flares of yellows, reds, or blues both to lure and purify him.

Meanwhile, from the bottom as a stoker and up, he worked on ships. When the furnace cooled too much, he stoked the coals into lighting up. Farther along the coast of Asia, he advanced on ship from stoker to trimmer as the ship splashed on to the harbor at Nagasaki. Whenever the ship's furnace required cooling, he'd shovel the embers, really clinkers, till they glowed. He, now the clinkerer, watered them, sissing to cool. Now again a trimmer, he pulverized impurities from the clumps. Waste gases wafted, half-asphyxiating him, as the ship floated into Tobo Bay.

* * *

After the bomb there and Japanese surrender, the commerce of peace and postwar resumed. Artie and other merchant seafarers began unloading and delivering the goods into Nagasaki itself. Soldiers in jeeps scrammed around the harbor. Armies of allies were occupying Japan. They would need khaki or olive uniforms, medicine, and fewer guns than earlier to patrol a bowed people.

Survivors, now captives, hid from the occupiers at first. Some few were swaddled in tatters. One, a boy of seven or eight, popped up beside Artie without bowing in custom to him, to see the big mariner. Scarred below his one eye, the boy jumped back into his sub-cellar home. When faced with any Westerner in khaki or blue uniforms, or civvies, the children usually fled.

The firestorm, heard about and aftereffects seen, caused runny heads or bodies. Which side of a head faced him? Artie spotted a boy who picked up someone's eye off the ground. After studying it, he threw it away. Another boy, taller than most, peeked out of his hideout at big Artie, loping by daily. In time, he trotted alongside Artie. Such kids Artie called, "Terrified little kids and terrorized souls who only want friends."

From supplies on his ship, Artie lifted cigarettes for grown-ups and suckers for kids. He handed out red and orange to ones he liked and greens. The children never smiled. Nor did they favor any color. Like little dogs clutching bones in their teeth, the children took their suckers and raced off. Farther on, they squealed while beaming the candy toward the sun, which shone through the colors.

* * *

With money earned, his paycheck raise, plus war bonus for risking the trip through torpedoes and enemy submarines, he could afford a leave. So, he hitched across Kyushu to the Inland Sea. He likened it to the Great Lakes waterway at home. He traveled toward Osaka and Kyoto. A grand barge, precursor of the grand tour boat line, accommodated him and others.

Stepping out of his black shoes, like all Japanese, and into scuffs the company supplied, he flip-flopped across the boat's threshold to the higher platform area. There, doffing them, he slipped into other scuffs. He toed them to the railing. Momentarily relaxing, he surveyed the water and rotated toward the boatload of persons, clumped in groups or askew. Each passenger seemed notched in an exact spot. From his point at the rail, he spotted a threesome on yellow tatami with enameled maroon flooring.

In a workaday rose kimono, a woman was pouring tea for an old man. A tan kimono draped another young woman. She sat rock-still. Her black obi crossed the full kimono. Raying across her shoulders to her waistband, her hair glossed black to reflect day in night.

Few Japanese women covered their hair by day. Only Catholics wore scarves, while trudging to church. At one, the Urakami Cathedral, the head of Christ, not just the thorns, was knocked off. Fat Boy, the bomb, split the head from the body of Jesus in the most Christian of Japanese cities, Nagasaki.

* * *

Here and now, on this passenger boat in a group close by his railing, this young woman swathed her head in a yellow runner above her kimono. Her face blurred. He, if rude, would have eyed her, but from back home, he heard his own mother still warning him. At this instant, he lowered his eyes in the Japanese manner. Unexpectedly, her scarf slipped off her silken hair and fell. He peeked, catching on to the melting and gelling of her face. She jerked her scarf back up. The fall of the scarf was a wink.

* * *

Suddenly, her mother tiptoed over to him by the railing. "Can I pour you tea?" He bowed and thanked her. At her urging, his long-sleeve pulled like a potholder over his hand under the teacup, so hot he dropped it on deck. "Sorry, sorry, so sorry." Unbroken and picked up, it welcomed more tea. "Thank you, thanks."

"No more tea left," the middle-aged Japanese woman returned to the ship deck with her threesome, daughter and father.

At the railing, blue shirt billowed in the sea breeze as the boat swayed. He felt clumsy trying to sip; his mother told him not slurp her tea. Where on the ocean was Pop? His mother?

The English of this Japanese woman dumbfounded him. He edged nearer her family and back to the railing. The horizon passed by.

Hesitant, he tried addressing, "*Okasan*," for Mrs. with Yamasaka. Later, he learned more formal, "*Haha*."

"Did America make you American or your family Nisei or Issei?"

"Can I figure it out? We spread out America before the war and spread after." Sighing, Haha poured him more tea. Her oldest married son lived in California, near her second son. By doing homework with an uncle outside the Nagasaki zone of attack, her third survived.

"The medical school of my brother's only son was 500 meters from the target. He and one hundred percent of students and teachers died there. Doctors and nurses race from towns to help Nagasaki. They help my daughter staying at home that day at zone edge.

"My Kumoi lives. I was outside the zone."

Kumoi's father believed still that China would float back to help them resettle. "My father," *Okasan* added, "leaves this boat at next stop. When times better, he arrange boys' marriages to Japanese girls. Oldest boy married his California-American girl. The other wants to. I, too, marry Californian." Okasan and Artie chit-chatted.

Scanning the water as the boat sped on, Artie tried out, "*sanyo-do*," for Inland Sea warmth. More filled out now than at the beginning of the war, his long voyage began easing into life on the floor and Kumoi.

His mother would have swatted him for staring at any cripple. So, he sat near her without looking. He moved his squatting muscles closer by.

In time, her mother commented, "The bomb: inferno like a volcano with earthquake fell from the sky to make islands of Japan."

So, too, the heat had scorched the rubble and burned

spotted people Artie witnessed in Nagasaki. The attack had loosened buildings. Crushed people, broke glass, and quashed thousands of people.

"After Americans attacked to end war," *Okasan* declared, "the mosquitoes followed. We itched. We cremated the dead for weeks. We scratched ourselves in the heat.

"The living dead, Kumoi, suffer nausea, diarrhea, and burning."

She jerked her head up. Her black eyes peered and blinked from under her long overhanging yellow scarf, shading her marred face. When the scarf was sliding off, her glossy, new black hair growth cascaded like calligraphy

In Nagasaki weeks on, he lugged rice, dry foods, and safe water to the Yamasakas. They were surviving with pumpkin skins, weeds, and potato vines. Eventually, they planted vegetables. *Okasan* also welcomed him into her home to measure and saw boards, level shelves, and replace bent screens.

Kumoi was silhouetted behind an opaque buff screen. Once, when Okasan left to market, Artie wound a red kerchief over his head to sop his sweat. Seeing only with his feet using scuffs to orient himself, he rose close to her so as not to scare her. At sixteen and nineteen, they might sound out each other through telepathy. They spoke no common language, nor could they touch because of her wounds.

Still, based in the wide Nagasaki harbor, he trekked to the public baths after the Yamasakas. At first, his bare buttocks plopped and skidded on the new, postwar yellow tile. Even Kumoi laughed at his awkwardness and joy. His nude belly was expanding from sake and beer. Steaming and scalding soothed every muscle, even ones in the lumbar area, ears, and head. Tension and ache departed. Calm swelled.

By letter home, he marveled. "Families, neighbors, and strangers sit together and soothe in the baths. Troubles never interfere." He himself loved the body Kumoi and the baths, more than the sea.

True, the bomb marred three-fourths of her face. Her shoulders above her breasts lay partially lifeless, but the rest of her was filled with life. Her elbows could swing beside her rib cage. The scarcity of food perfected her. In sly moments, without Haha knowing, he began holding her.

* * *

By the end of his stay with the Americans, and alongside the Australians, he was serving as a ship clinkerer-trimmer in the Nagasaki harbor. Impure chunks from his ship's furnace goal he mixed into poor cement. From this work, he grew lean again.

Returning months later from Japan to New York City, Artie spun out his Nagasaki tales and regaled them to any listener, including his brother Will. World War II framed Artie's life; Vietnam would for Will.

For their mother, Artie's birth had marked the onset of her adult life. Back from Asia, when he was scouring want ads for work, his mother reminded him that with his talents he could do many jobs, take care of anybody.

"In fact, when you were a kid, you could have gone on the Broadway stage."

Bass notes voiced from his belly. "Okasan, don't start up."

"Just suggesting ways to go."

"What?" No time for the stage mother role or gofer, had she. His mother geared her sons for "early independence," instilling does and don'ts, and relied on her brother, who knew the ropes. "Your uncle guided you, little Artie, chubby star with baby charisma, you were, to tryouts."

"I'm not one now and I'm not interested in Broadway."

Eventually though, his uncle, her brother, became too infirm to help care for Artie's younger brother Willie. By the time he found an assistant super's job, their mother prompted, "Go up to see big Artie."

Originally, their father was Big Artie. He was nowhere to be found at this point.

So, it fell to Artie II to look after Will. "Take the Broadway line to 72 Street stop and walk toward the river." To eight-year-old Willie, she noted, "Read the signs. Your brother got to Japan and back. You'll get somewhere. You think you're alone in life. Plenty of others are going the same way you are. Ask and they'll tell you the way to find Artie's place."

"Take me," Willie begged.

She refused, as Artie knew she would. "His paintings hang in his front hall. I know my nude self too well, dips, lines, extra bumps. I don't want to see his nude paintings."

* * *

At his door, Artie patted the boy's reddish brush cut, and ushered him into his apartment. In his rooms, Artie displayed his present and past. From his brother's seagoing, Willie spotted mementos, nude and nautical. A sea- and salt-encrusted anchor lay on the floor at a slant. Will called it "a fallen cross or weather-vane down from a tornado."

Next to his brown couch, for his mugs of coffee, clear tea, and beer, a flat-topped lighthouse beacon served as his coffee table. "Turn it on."

"No." Artie egged Willie on. "If lit up close, it could blind you." Instead, Artie lit up a hanging copper boat lantern. "You can have it."

Willie ignored the offer. He stared through his uncle's telescope out the window. "This is what I want," he told his uncle.

After Nagasaki, while at sea, Artie painted with oils on boards or sailcloth for canvases. He'd included likenesses of Kumoi that Willie gazed at, but said nothing about to Mom.

Toward dusk, big Artie rode elevator with small Willie to use the telescope on the heavens. Artie admonished him ahead of the viewing. "Don't point it at the sun or sunset, the heavens. It's all pieces. Gravity joins atoms for the hardest-to-see naked-eye star. Like a volcano close to us." They telescoped down-river the Ports of New York and faraway Nagasaki neither could see.

In the portrait of memory, back in the apartment, dull orange, yellow, cream, and chartreuse by vermilion layered up Kumoi. He'd perfected his Kumoi paintings enough to hang the best on the wall.

Reaching adolescence, Willie taunted his brother, "You'll never see her again." But Artie wrote Kumoi's mother.

"Wait and see. Don't knock my painting. I'm no Hiroshige, but I'll paint another."

Willie sneered. "She'll swim the Pacific for you?"

Artie pounded his medicine ball at Willie. In a better job now, he transferred to a building giant to help manage and superintend.

Days afterward, Eddie sauntered in and sat down next to Artie, celebrating his new job at the Seahorse, their waterside haunt, where they'd first met off-ship. Still in his U.S. army crew cut, his buddy called himself, "American-Japanese." At the time, hardly anyone noticed them.

From island nation origins, Artie off Europe and Eddie off Asia, Artie followed his father into the army; Eddie wound up interned with his father in Camp Pinedale in California. Let out, he joined the all-Japanese U.S. army regiment.

Here at the Seahorse counter, the two vets ribbed each other over war tales and food. Artie's mother plopped mashed potatoes on a plate and Eddie's patterned rice and greens on one, maybe with a hibiscus.

After the war, Eddie introduced his future Caucasian-American wife to his mother, an Issei. She reacted, "Never."

* * *

Three years later, Okasan Yamasaki allowed her Kumoi with the melted face to travel. Artie proposed she join a plastic surgery tour, like one from Hiroshima. Medical philanthropists would help her reshape her face in New York.

After three surgical rounds, she sat with Eddie, who translated for her. No longer ultra-shy and faceless, Kumoi told Eddie, “I am going to give birth to a baby.”

Eddie was perplexed. “Announcing your plan is not how you go about giving birth.”

“With you, I will." Kumoi pressed to stay on with Eddie.

"But I have a wife!"

"But you could have a Japanese wife."

"No." Knowing that his existing wife and Artie were losing out, Eddie sought to exchange with him, easing him back in. Artie slogged on.

Learning English, self-care, and sewing, she repaired kimonos, Western clothes, and designed some for a shop. She earned enough to maintain herself.

Of all her peers, the medical committee adored Kumoi most, yet little knew her self-will. Eddie caught on that she was denying his Western wife’s reality. Actively, he edged Artie back into the picture.

After all, Artie could fix anything. He could build shelves and straighten warped floors. He improved Kumoi’s room in the committee’s apartment suite. Doing so, he again grew more than fond of the petite woman with her new pert nose by her same eyes between puffy bangs and cheeks.

Her split curls pasted near her re-formed earlobes, aligned with her mouth. She added hairstyling to her work repertoire.

She confided in one who gossiped to a philanthropic

committee member about her wish for a baby. At that time, the press was snooping around her fellow maidens. In case of possible lapse into pregnancy, the committee ordered her home.

* * *

Suggestive of the matter, her mother wrote back to Artie. Kumoi had met another American from the still occupying forces there ....

Though his colors were now muted rather than the earlier bright choices, more canvases emerged. They shaded into Kumoi, beguiling him.

* * *

Owners of Artie's hangout, the Seahorse, had paneled it with pine and cut portholes near the ceiling by the time Artie brought Will in. They sat at one side of the U-shaped bar, while Artie held forth. "They don't make stars with faces anymore. Hollywood stars look like everyone else. No za-za glamor, no great lookers, just run-on faces, anybody's, paper blow-ups, no Gables or Garbos."

Artie belted down two boilermakers, dribbled on his red and gray shirt, and puffed two cigarettes down to their filters. Coming from the john, Will saw the barstool held up big Artie like a mushroom and told him so.

Artie ignored Will for a regular who'd arrived to jaw with.

"You guys stay," Will said, "I'm going."

"Restless to go live?!"

Will grew restless for his own life, not replayed lies, made-up lives, or the good old days via Artie's boilermakers and George's black Russians. Artie the colorist said George's pewter hair clashed with his copper skin. Artie spotted himself gleaming in the high polish of the dark-stained wooden counter and joked, "See me now in the wood." George, Will, and Eddie, who'd come in, groaned.

They praised their luck. Typically, George would pipe up. "Thank God we were on a merchant ship. There's no freedom on an ammo ship. It's one prison, which if you're on leave and late, they throw you in the brig."

They debated their luck in missing Japanese sub attacks, while floating toward Japan to rescue the Japanese from themselves in 1945. Artie declared, "Could have landed before the bomb instead of afterward. Your grandfather washed up after World War II here in New York City, the Seahorse."

"The baths."

"Not quite. Foam, true. Well, during Prohibition, he'd send me here down the block with a couple of half-gallon buckets, growlers. The bartender'd fill it with foam from a spout under the counter. Then, I'd take them back up to Grandpa and Dad."

More somber with each growler, Artie was recalling his lasts: the last time he saw his old man, the last time their Mom worked on her world map puzzle.

"The last time," Will said, "you saw your Lady of Nagasaki who deserted you."

"Faithful as Mom," Artie retorted.

"One of your lesser geishas, not Mom." Will gulped down a growler of Seahorse foam.

Artie was piecing together what he knew, "Could a woman stall off a male boarder?" The Seahorse joviality rolled surly, as Artie pieced events together. He was starting to believe that back from the war at sea, his Pop, broke as usual, was counting on his war risk bonus against a blow-up at sea, not charity.

"Nobody here likes charity," he said. "He grabbed work to get by on and was stranded with war injuries in one of Tojo's prison camps. To pay the bills, Mom took in a boarder. When I returned to New York, she was carrying a baby. I left."

"That was you, Will."

"Our father I never knew was yours only?"

The bartender was thumping the bar with his knuckles.

* * *

In their third period, twenty years later, the second in New York, Artie hoped to put Kumoi at ease. Evidently, she planned to set him straight.

Back in Nagasaki, her family reassembled. Her father had rejoined them from China in 1946 though soon died. Soon after, she'd met an American soldier, and within her mother's doubt, she'd married the Californian. Oddly enough, her siblings landed back in Nagasaki. In due time, her husband lapsed from her for a fellow Caucasian. So Kumoi slipped away from her first San Francisco home into her second in the Mission.

Ceaselessly, her lapsed husband tried luring her back. Implacable, she welcomed only her Eurasian sons to her apartment.

* * *

In New York for the second time, she framed and mounted photos of her sons. Artie hung them.

She declared, "Now alone at last. I am the artist." Her Lower East Side apartment, embellished with screens and cushions on tatami, reminded him of First Okasan's home. Her mother had banned shiny surfaces and covered their windows with blinds to eliminate reflecting Kumoi's youthful facelessness. At her homecoming from New York surgery, her mother restored mirrors. Windows which reflected Kumoi also faced their household garden in Nagasaki.

Here in a New York hotel hair salon, she excelled in asymmetrical styles. For his cut around the ears, he refused her mirror to double-check her work and she his paying her.

In her studio, he hesitated while admiring her Technicolor canvases. Both hairstyles and paintings were earning her some local Lower East Side renown as a stylist.

Under her circular, when sitting, or semi-circular bright skirts, or when standing with the sides fanned out from her hands, she fit the times. On her yardage for skirts, she silk-screened great balls of fire in yellow, red, or green, in time, modulated into mauve, rose, pearl white, ivory, and others he thought monochromatic and dull. She circled her neck with black Mikimoto cultured pearls.

To her sneezing, he uttered, "God bless you. Bless you."

"We don't say that in Japanese," she said, fingering her pearls.

Gazing upon her décor, he told her, "Little real color. Also, your doorknobs are loose or falling off. You need someone to hold onto."

"When I was young," she said, "I was trusting. I've lived some number of years. So, my brother writes to ask, 'Who will care for me, when I am old?' When the time comes, I will go home.

"People there still find growths on their bodies from the bombs' old gamma rays, still radiating.

"You never know, you too may find them. You were there."

* * *

Nagasaki rippled into Kumoi. Artie stayed less in New York and more by the sea, Sheepshead Bay, Oyster Bay, and farther out on Long Island. Along the shore, he watched fisherman toss their nets to seine the Sound waves. Oyster fishing, love of clamming, rowing, sailing, swimming, snorkeling, scuba diving, he relished, "Anything to do with the sea." So, in a catamaran or a sailboat smaller than his size, the waves rocked him out on the Sound.

Once in the milky haze at dusk, he lost his way in a rowboat, until a coast guard cutter rescued him. Chance little deterred him. Still he dove into the depths and rose through the sub-surface to the surface, returning to life at sea.

Cut to Fit

Twenty others waited ahead of me at the service counter, when I arrived on this Line W. From its head, a tall woman, tinseled blond and dressed in cerise, charged past me and griped. "I don't believe this line, this line. From losing my job, I got a runaround that deserves a 'bestseller.'"

Sucked to the back of the room where sent, she whooshed. Now only three persons ahead of me, an older African-American man boomed, "Lady, you do that. Put in your book, it's five weeks since I got laid off and still no unemployment check. I got to get me some cash." Taller than most and fit with care into his brown business suit, he let out a singsong, "A wife, a wife would be so nice."

Now 19 claimants stood ahead of me on our Line W that jiggled and tittered to his jingle. Someone unseen retorted, "A wife could help, if her money's coming in."

On the Line E, a tall Latina jested to us, "On this damn line, you should fall in love to find a rent share." Because of her glamour, black glossed hair, and long, svelte, moss green dress smoothed over a curvy body, she caught Line W eyes.

From my pocket, I pulled five Canadian dollars and silver coins from my last summer's vacation with my then-boyfriend and called him about them. I'd scrounged the money from my bureau drawer to exchange for U.S. money.

No, he saved none in his drawers, he said, that I could borrow. Not only that, his paycheck got caught in his office's computer, so he can't help me out.

We'd agreed to leave each other, because we were over the loss of our last lover-companions, yes, indeed, so we didn't need each other as a lean-to anymore. He was not sure what he wanted. I wasn't either. We really broke up over loose change.

While missing him, I'd been juggling certain decisions. Should I buy health food store yogurt without chemicals or granola. To preserve my health or do without, could I eat just two lunches next week? A friend of mine, an artist from an old Yankee family she no longer benefits from that made part of its money from slavery, sized-up her dilemma as a choice between buying supper or new underpants, panties, that is. I just faced the dilemmas, so I tried to wait tables off the books.

Meanwhile, the Latina sang out, "The time's so long here with so many foul-ups, someone could start a start-up. Even a food cart could earn pennies." When she turned, the comedy and tragedy masks on her silver-plated choker gleamed.

On the line, I've spent hours, not money, applying for benefits. I've been trying to revise my benefit claim upward. Along with my old pay stubs, I've brought in my tax form. The authorities say they've been converting from paper use to computers, so we won't have to stand much longer or stand in the unemployment line. You can sit at your computer to apply for unemployment benefits.

Off the line or online, I've been meditating on how to get by on next to nothing. Stay calm, no matter what. Be kind. You never know who you'll meet. Breathe. Because my mental health remains a little at stake, I have to network, because the mental health clinic that laid me off cannot call me back as an art therapist. A friend still there told me that someone laid off from the city government has resumed her first career and bumped me forever from my job line.

Here state labor rules demand we dress ready for work. On line, most have worn jeans or clothes in official navy or park green. A few of us garbed ourselves in drab. Like a misfit, my togs were mismatched, gray and navy makeshift.

My mother, who visited me, told me I'm like a displaced person from her day, and my apartment's a tenement. To go with my outfit, my brown hair has sprigged into a style of many lengths.

Us claimants fidgeted as we closed in on the counter. The clerk on its other side humored the older black man up ahead. "I was jobless too once for seven months."

The older man pooh-poohed him. "I was unemployed once for seven years." At his comeback, the Line W bobbed with glee. He vented, “Tomorrow's my sixty-first birthday. Think they'll let me retire?"

Graying at the temples, a professorial type on the Line W across from me on the Line E looked up at our to-do. I squinted at the headlines of his newspaper. They indicate downsizing was leading to an upturn that will land in a gentle downturn that will emerge into a turnaround. Things the newspapers have been trying to spell out as worsening are now improving.

Next, I overheard the type like a professor talk about breakdown and buildup. When he said he was down from the Yukon, another tall, thin fellow behind me with black wire glasses and a violin case injected, "I hear they wiped out social sciences at the U. of Conn." I caught on, except to econ.

Also, the pliancy of the linoleum floor, checkered in black and red, eased our footsteps, forever dense in this acre of room, imprinted by claimants. The opaque ceiling of soundproofed squares with holes muffled our words in this Park Row building office.

Some of us tried to out-shout the room's silencing. A guard shushed our hullabaloo. She bore traces of epaulettes, without stars, buttoned-down on the shoulders of her uniform, and a chrome badge. This big woman commanded us. "Quiet. Straighten your line!" We did so.

After two hours of waiting to reach the front of W, the clerk announced to the sixty-one-year-old man, "If you want, you can go for temporary assistance." The older guy shouted back on his way out, "Happy Birthday!"

We started up singing, "Happy Birthday" to him. The guard shouted, "Quiet."

* * *

Twenty years ago, we teenaged farm laborers woke at about 4:00 a.m. to catch the 6:00 truck at our town limits to work under the corn. Like palm trees, its plants shaded us. But its leaves could cut us when high corn stalks we had to stretch to reach their tassels. Removing the corn tassels avoided self-pollinating by the stamen. De-tasseling bettered the hybrid seed corn.

Once in the fields, if lucky, we hopped on a giant metal locust of a farm machine some would call a butterfly that crawled over eight rows of corn at once. Otherwise, we walked in the bitter heat. Riding also meant less work pulling tassels up and off the plants.

My mother voiced her distaste for my activity and urged her 1930s Depression Mentality on me, then aged 13, and my sister. "Keep only the lights you need on," she reminded us. "Another thing; wear that 'old,' as you call it, red cotton sweater another year. Don't bunch or stretch it. It'll be fine."

Nevertheless, I would use my first real earnings to buy a cashmere sweater, a real one. By means of my string of odd jobs, in time, a yarn of acrylic got pulled through my cashmere. While I worked for extras, my truck mates worked for basics.

"Your great grandfather's and grandfather's small-town bank," my mother, a Republican, commented to test us, "lasted in the Depression because of such economies." Because she valued hard work and handwork as fine efforts, she kept her ambivalence about my new work to herself. My father, a Democrat, agreed. While others in my family tried neutrality, my older sister belittled my new farm work. I told her to keep her mug out of my business. My father reacted, "Watch out."

Teen Albanians shared our insect or locust wing for detasseling, if possible, to avoid being knocked down in the fields. Italians said the

Albanians pretended when they arrived here to be Italians. Otherwise, they might face taunts and be knocked down.

* * *

A few years later, I lucked out with a grad school fellowship in art therapy. Last time, my friend Sally met on the line in faded jeans, told me she's getting her master's, and her professor informed her that her unemployment benefits surpassed any fellowship he knew of for grad school.

Here on the line, I was teetering from one foot to another for three-and-a-half hours until I could slump, like the others in front of me, on the gray Formica counter. It divided the unemployed from the employed clerks and officials. I reacted to everyone around me and couldn't focus on the book I brought to commiserate with myself in New York, George Orwell's DOWN AND OUT IN LONDON AND PARIS, but I tried.

As I managed to move closer in line to the front clerk, I strained my eyes over a poster on the far wall reading, "YOU ARE A WISE, CREATIVE, strong, clever, discriminating, refined... " until the letters disappeared.

Behind me, the twentyish-year-old dark-haired man with black wire glasses and a mustache stood upright. His name unknown. One of the genteel poor, I figured, who carried a violin case. So, I asked, "Are you an out-of-work violinist?"

To answer, he opened his case, in case I thought him an old bootlegger or drug dealer. Empty, its lush, dark red lining impressed me. He snapped the case shut.

Testily, he said, "I went to the violin repairer. But they'll rap my knuckles here for not going to the employment office last week. Without a violin, how can I prove I'm trying to work?"

He'd better not use a lame excuse. "Last year," I sympathized, "some say they were more civil here; this year they want you to feel your worth with a job." A film editor friend, I explained to the violinist, felt hassled. An official yelled at her for bringing her baby to the line. But her sitter had come down with gallstones, and my friend could no longer afford the sitter anyway.

"You come to this line for a job in music?" I asked.

"You don't," he snapped. His dark mustache twitched. "I proofread, until 82 of us got laid off. Too many English majors stay in publishing."

Another unemployment claimant was reading, A WOMAN'S GUIDE TO A SUCCESSFUL CAREER. I wondered about the age of that book.

Line W was moving faster, compared with our E. So, and a coach appeared across from me. His heavy brow was pleating, and his light brown hair angled out like antennae. A coach and English teacher, he told me, “Half our staff was dismissed this year. We're supposed to teach double the number of students to run and read double-time without being in the school. Not only that, last year we arranged for 13 athletic scholarships for college. Now no one'll do them." His duffle bag bore Rosen ... something on it I could not read. Rosencrantz?

"What now?" I asked.

"Sales."

Finally, I reached the counter and was nervous when the clerk asked to see my last year's W-2 tax form for my work as an art therapist in a community mental health center. She sent me back to the back of the room.

At last, I could sit. Now I spotted another pep-up sign. "If you see someone without a smile, give him one of yours." Imagine the coach or violinist-proofreader smiling. Already, I missed them.

You get used to people on the line, and, then, they go away. Still the woman in the cerise dress, already in the back for two hours, was skipping lunch and reading, THE WOMAN'S GUIDE TO BEAUTY. How else could she spiff herself up like a fashionista? What could she do to spruce herself? Her diamond needed polishing, I noted, as she was saying, "Too many people in this city get by on welfare and extra help nobody else gets." Also, her forefinger nail's maple nut polish was chipping and needed another coat.

In the meantime, others from my line came back from lunch. The coach informed me, "The split pea soup next door is very good."

The ex-consultant confided, had just added an architect and a lawyer. "Everybody comes here sooner or later," the cerise-dressed woman, named Celeste, commented.

In a dark suit and topcoat, the lawyer was citing a pocket BARTLETT'S FAMILIAR QUOTATIONS. "Poor naked wretches, where're you are, That bide the pelting of this pitiless storm, ... o, house-less heads, and unfed sides.... " This lawyer was seeking precedents.

* * *

Over the holidays, some friends invited me to parties with ample food. At my first party, the Sunday before Christmas, my older friend Phoebe met me at the door in her shocking pink dress with dazzling crystal rainbow earrings to go with her new platinum hair dye. She introduced me around to the others and to Octavia, her old friend; her hard-of-hearing great uncle George, a retired economist from the Federal Reserve Board; Peter, her cousin's nephew, worked as the same for the same. Whenever Peter spoke, I planned to cock my ear for clues about the economy.

For air, I seated myself next to the window and adjacent to Aunt Julia, dressed in rose jersey, cut on the bias. She sat on the settee and lived on Sutton Place. I wished at that moment that I'd chosen the punch with the alcohol, as she was saying, "Times have changed. My children now have to make choices."

If I could room at her place and care for her in her old age and her old mutt, Socrates, as Phoebe is doing with her great uncle who'd maybe brought along his $3-400,000, I could create a life for myself.

Covering all fronts, I next made a point to sit next to my own hard-of-hearing great uncle, who agreed with all I said to him. He offered possibilities, until Mariah blew in.

Her father was a Lebanese banker, and her mother was the daughter of one in Zurich. En route to another, fancier party, Mariah came dressed in silver lame under her black fur. For a decade, she'd worked as a refinancing expert in Singapore for a worldwide firm.

These facts I knew because she'd consulted with me about her young son's artistic ability. To retain her post and manage her marriage and mother, she visited her son every twenty-eight days. Recently, she arrived to stay put in New York and launched her own start-up company on her beeper from her basement, which she planned to upgrade to a cell phone.

She has been living in a basement apartment in Phoebe's building. At the latter's party, Mariah placed herself on the other side of hard-of-hearing great uncle. He nodded, agreeing more with her than with me. So

Mariah has the edge over me.

* * *

At the second holiday party, my buddy Joey, an artist not an art therapist like me, asked me to his loft to spend Christmas dinner with some friends. His loft windows overlook the Empire State Building. At Joey's very narrow dining table, a door on barrels, I dined across from a youngish Scotsman, named Jamie or Jeremy. I thought about his prospects or mine.

Gazing into my eyes, he said, "Oh, you really listen. I'm happy to be in a crowd like this." His long pigtail matched his dark tan sports jacket. When he reached for the wine, his stretch revealed a hole in his sunburst tie-dye T-shirt that I'd thought had gone out of style, but was brought back in favor in line with my mother's line of thought on recycling.

How we got on the topic of hash, I'm not sure, except some of my clinic clients smoked it. I never would, of course. "Yes, I used to," he said, "sell it in Central Park."

Did coke use to be part of his menu, I asked him. "Yes, yes." Heroin?

"No, never heroin. You could rake in," he said, "a lot of hay in Central Park in the old days, easy money." When his toes started to touch mine under the table, I figured out he had holes in his socks, like his T-shirt, and was prey to athlete's foot. I could get it, while playing footsie. So, I ruled him out as a possibility.

The following Sunday during the holidays, I prayed in church for a better world. On one side sat my friend Edie, who's an academic logician. She has the mid-life blues. But she possesses a post in life and a husband.

With neither one, I qualify for the blues.

On my other side though sat a political scientist, tall and handsome, dark-eyed. He kept edging down the pew toward me. Because he speaks some Japanese and German, he shows actual promise, and is working on Russian and Arabic. But he owes it to himself to finish his book, so he can obtain a university post and at least a studio larger than the room in the church steeple, where he lives now.

On Boxing Day, I somehow went to a party of diplomats from the British Commonwealth. Nothing happened.

At a New Year's Eve party, just when my benefits ran out, I ran into Sally in a short skirt this time. She'd had a run of luck with a temp job and said, "You catch your benefits on the phone and computer now." My phone service was cut off; so was my computer.

Coming and going from parties on and around New Year's, I kept passing the homeless on a bench by the triangle, a garden fenced in and locked up. With a long gray pigtail, one often sat reading, my neighbor pointed out to me, fat medical books. For months, I'd seen the men there, maybe years, but little-noticed them.

On New Year's Day in the cold rain, I hauled my tin cans to the supermarket to redeem them instead of leaving them for Artie's superintendent's assistant to cart away. Between one stray shopping cart and a cracked glass over a framed pheasant print, its guardian slept with soaked blankets over his body and head. His soul must have been dry.

Earlier, I'd dismantled my little Christmas tree and boxed up my gold and silver cherubs and white doves that once decorated it. Back from the store and at home, I took the red oilcloth from around the tree base back down the street and lay it over the human being.

The next day when I was walking by him, he was

standing. He winked at me out of his right eye and saluted me with his right hand. I nodded. The red oilcloth was hanging over the bench next to the gold pheasant. I thought to myself, he might just be okay. We could live in the caves across the street in the park. After all, natives had lived there in the Hill Park caves until the end of the 1930s Depression. Carrying my bowl around, I could seek and ease myself onto our new path.

Gyring on the Edge

Along the coast of China, the plane rocked over the sea. She feared the plane would crash. Without special plans, beyond a simple visa, you could rarely get into China in those days. Now she was plotting to reach Asia.

Wary of an emergency landing in the ocean, she, shackled in her seat, jerked her head around. Couples nestled. A western baby whimpered. An Asian baby slept. Other passengers were chattering in several tongues. She pried out a name here and there during the long flight.

During the overthrow of the emperor, Sun Yat-sen, unifier and father of the republic, called for Mandarin. Outside the port of Hong Kong, Chinese spoke Cantonese. With another swoop of the wings, words clattered and muttered.

Where were they, in what area and language? The woman ahead, in her loosened seat belt, bent around the high back of her chair. In the tongue of her Macau island birth and accented with precise English, she addressed both the woman across the aisle and Nan behind her.

Across from Nan sat a fellow whose features ranged in even thirds—forehead, nose and mouth-chin—along his profile. He'd entered the plane at Taipei. He was reading his magazine page by page. Yet in one grand dive of the plane, their eyes seemed to bump toward each other's. She snatched a view of his stoic and handsome face. To ignore the turbulence around them, he returned to his business magazine. Abruptly, he rotated back to her and pointed to a picture, "It's You."

Nan hid that she knew herself in the photo. After this sit-in months ago, she was going out to look at the war zone that generated the sit-in. "Maybe. You don't see yourself, what you look like. I don't."

"Isn't this a likeness?" he asked.

The woman in front of Nan and kitty-corner from his chair agreed with him. Like passengers, they were distracting themselves from the tipsy plane trip in any way. The thirtyish Chinese woman, westernized in a plaid sleeveless blouse with black pants, nodded to her young daughter and to Nan.

On their way to Hong Kong, he noted with Nan that it was "the world's smuggler capital." The woman from Macau agreed.

Then he was going on to Beijing for pandas or other bears. With a downdraft of the plane, he grinned. A Washington, D.C. zoo trustee, he talked on and squeezed the woman from Macau's hand. His reddish-brown hair raveled around his ears and high, squared forehead. "Come with me."

Once more, the plane zoomed down to outflank the wind. Nan grabbed a paper bag in case she barfed and quivered over the uncertainty that played within her, wishing her father, Will, were here. "I'll let you know."

The flight calm again, passengers chattered. On her other side, an American commercial pilot, round-faced, ruddy, talked. "Stay away from the cities. They're Chinese. Meet real Thais, real Vietnamese? Wade out to people of the paddies."

Eventually though, students on the plane, bound for

their Land of Smiles, egged her onto a plan. Stretching and walking on the aisle, she mingled and heard about the oldest part of cities. Their centers, whether Bangkok or Chieng Mai, she gathered, belonged to the real Indo-Chinese.

The plane swooped as the young mother from Macau was listening in to the Thai students. Wiggling her fore and index fingers over the high back of her plane chair, the young mother ahead who lived in Chicago vouched for Kuan-Yin, Goddess of Mercy, against turmoil. It led a Vietnamese woman, while seated, to bow down with hands praying. Asked, she recommended for all nearby on the plane to venerate *Lay Mu.*

Back in her seat, Nan dreamed of inner gardens while the plane coasted. Along the klongs, the canals, between the avenues, onto the rungs. Those alleys, they say, have alcoves with all wares. Pass between the stalls and kiosks. Taste the tang of Thai delicacies, tidbits spiked with leek or sweets or lemongrass. Drape yourself in garlands of jasmine and wear sarongs. Royal blue awnings will shade you from sun, rain, and harm. Go on farther into those caves to see silks and thongs for daily changes from room to room, outer to inner. Move on through to temples of gold. Surrender unto serenity.

As its passengers began packing up to disembark, they slipped their arms through backpacks, like donning parachutes ready to unleash. Pull the string, ready to go. All belonged to one streamer. From its one reality, they could swing into another paradise.

* * *

From the plane above, Bangkok stretched out like Washington, D.C. Once on the ground, Bangkok looked parched; D.C., bleached. Landing in *Krung Shep*, native for Bangkok, a city of angels, a vague look-alike for Los Angeles. The autos' honking exhaust harangued her from one landmark to the next. After the monsoon, the city was drying up. Its grit and dust in khaki color nettled her. However, lapped by the paddies from the Central Plain, Bangkok stoked up like a dessert within an oasis.

Usually, upon arrival at any capital she poked along the streets to seek out what she needed and how people reacted. In Tokyo, Japanese had nodded or bowed slightly and interrupted their scurrying to gesture and point to a map for her way forth. So, her hopes for the same thronged toward Bangkok.

Stilled by the heat, she was little bothered about whether the city smiled upon her from airport to rail station. She and two others crossed klongs, canals, and avenues to search for a hotel. They slunk toward a bin of a hotel, cheapest and nearest to the city center. Automobiles through here clogged the streets and her lungs, exhausting her, as she was discovering. At first, the hostel was thought meant for youth. The huge room they checked into held rows of cots on the scale of a gym armory.

From her gray canvas bag, she pulled out and on her pale green cotton nightgown, net-like for air. She blew up her air mattress, tied down her white silk parachute sheet, and crawled inside its pocket. But in the night heat, its sides and the sheets stuck to her body.

Once her nightgown untwisted enough, she struggled to stay on her mattress and off the hostel one beneath, with it the dried goo of bought sex.

After all, she should have gone off with the trustee.

Next dawn, before the light or the awakenings of her would-be traveling companions from the plane, she slipped out early and squinted at the city. Khaki figures walked around. A war was going on somewhere.

Maybe no one would catch on to her. Because of her off-black eyes and thick dark hair, some people here might take, or had taken, her for Asian, and leave her alone as invisible.

Once too, a laughing time ago, a male friend, reaching for her, had removed his glasses, to demonstrate that he like her, half-Hungarian, bore eyes from ancestry that had long ago raced across the Asian infinity of steppes. Recently, in Japan, some people, if down and out and un-tuned in, spoke to her in Japanese.

Whether poor, or better off, some had poured tea for her. Another family had extended their meal for her. Next, she and a German woman from their hostel strolled in a park of unequaled beauty, a giant bonsai-like garden between Tokyo and Hiroshima. Dozens of Koreans, rather than Japanese, pursued her and her temporary fellow back-packer, not, as it turned out, because they looked Asian. Instead this convention of men wished for photos of American women. Her Uncle Artie had never fought the North Koreans. What would he think? She and the other woman, Mae, posed for small payback for all the half-and-half babies from the other way around in wartime. After snapping their cameras, the Koreans had bowed in unison.

* * *

Weeks later, in a Bangkok hostel, lizards tched-tched overhead. In Cambodia's dusk, they were quieter than in Thailand. Where she lived, boys scared girls. Here they were keeping her stupefied with fatigue. What if they lost their minuscule grips on the rough stucco-like ceiling?

Meanwhile her half-Chinese, half-Indian roommate was brushing her black hair to shimmer above her deep rose sari. Before going out for the evening, she told Nan a tale.

Once, while taking tea, the Asian woman's legs twitched surprisingly. Out leaped a lizard. She smiled at Nan. "Lizards are harmless." She snapped out the light and closed the door behind her. The musk and Channel No. 5 combo wafted after her. Nan burrowed in, praying the lizards would stay on the ceiling. In quasi-haze, they loomed into crocodiles and alligators, a leviathan overtaking her.

* * *

In the morning, a Chinese café in Bangkok, found almost anywhere and not honored in any guidebook, bolted her into the day, she was sure. Shuttling among tables, refrigerator, kitchen, and counter, the waiter took Asians chopsticks and big spoons to go with their tea, soup, and rice. She herself received a knife, fork, spoon, and napkin with her eggs.

Then, someone turned on overhead fans, *punkahs,* whose propellers stirred the sullen dawn for some relief. Sleepiness lingered. Hustle in the café was moving everywhere like minutia. Atoms were shivering, until she woke up enough to see the whole.

The café floor edged out to the sidewalk, its frets angled at one another outside up and down the street, long before the streetwalkers or students arrived, Workers were spitting and rushing by or in, as shopkeepers yanked open metal doors and gates, allowing lottery hawkers to flock into the café. Following them, beggars spilled in. Those in this café belonged not to the saffron-robed or brown-red orders of monks. Some though held out bowls for coins. Travelers favored them.

One shaved-headed man refused alms to a beggar woman. She tossed her maybe lice-ridden hair over his table. Here more beggars thrust themselves like mortar into the café only to be ejected with "scat" sounding words.

Back in the whitewashed compound, she focused on the older woman in charge, her sturdiness dipped in her chocolate-colored wrap, *paisin*. Thai? Malay? From her bright, all-seeing eyes and heart mouth, she asked Nan, "Why up so early?"

"Excitement: Bangkok and lizards, monkeys kept me awake."

"They're harmless, more fearful of you than you are of them." Mrs. Ranga ridiculed by trying to describe lizards' suctions for inside walls and agility of dark monkeys cavorting, both never falling.

Jovial, Mrs. Ranga ordered all. "Drop your keys at the front desk and Nan, watch out for boys."

Feeling meddled with, denied of good judgment, Nan went back to the desk to ask for Mae. She was expected to arrive any moment from Tokyo, where she had stayed with her brother. The owner-manager found no sign of her. Nan went and sank back into a deck chair, lolling there, brooding. Was this Mrs. Ranga? The roommate of Nan had whispered about her low enough almost to match the s-s-s-of the groups of lizards. Identified as a gambler at her favorite casino, Mrs. Ranga got into her business by procuring, wasn't that the word, the services of a twelve-year-old girl to pay off her gambling debts. That was the rumor among the girls in the compound.

Within the compound grew wild and tame magnolia, geraniums, and roses, roses in yellow, pallor and gaudier shades beneath and among the feathery palms. Bougainvillea draped high and beyond them. A sparrow flew across her view to join fellow sparrows at the far end of the park.

Someone was intruding in on Nan's thoughts on how to travel North in Thailand. The legs of a man, whose dark brown hair was longish in the front, slipping onto his face, gulped the distance between the compound gate and her chair.

"Welcome to Thailand," he said, throwing his hair back from his head, more English than American. "What brings you here?" They exchanged names of Jim Ripley and Nan Marvin, as if at a party with others coming and going.

In this Asian Eden, he tensed and grew restless, evidently waiting for someone and not listening. No, the buzzer, Nan realized, was for the woman in the sari, because another man crossed the yard. Nan had tut-tutted with her the evening before. Ripley, the fellow nearby, stood up, and appeared vexed at a nonappearance.

Was he rankling over the tiny Asian Nan had

glimpsed in their room?

By hearing, in spite of his edginess, that Nan was aiming for the North of Thailand, India, and Nepal, he declared, “I plan to hit those places someday."

First, she wished to go North in Thailand with someone, if Mae refused to go. Temporary companions were available from Asian guest houses. To her hint he accompany her, he replied, “You’re right nowadays not to go alone. Too lonely. I work up there. Be sure to go up there." He invited her only into the idea of leaving Bangkok. “Fly to Chieng Mai, Rose of the North, virgin territory with teak forests and flowers."

He would eye, she believed, a tree of gardenias, like Thais in crystal. Unable to choose one, he would pluck all of them.

She announced, “I'm taking the train North; you can meet people,” she’d heard, “on a third-class train." He grinned and said. “Cheaper fare than on a plane, for sure. Maybe you should hitch.” She giggled. He was mocking her way of the road: that backpacked, kept costs down, contacts up, and knew few maps. Points of the compass to follow were left to chance.

“You’re right not to go it alone the fancy way.” He urged her to go to the more Thai than Chinese areas, like Bangkok, where merchants buy licenses from the government to use Chinese on their shop signs.

At that moment, Mae, another traveler, arrived and sat down as Jim Ripley was launching his lesson: Thais, once partly Chinese, sprang from Mongolia, settled in China in the sixth century and arrived in Indochina in the twelfth. Then filtered in the true Chinese. Until a hundred years ago, they’d operated Thai trade and served as its tax and customs collectors. Still, they operated most stores and held most skilled jobs. The Dutch, he went on, especially the English, and even the French and Americans, helped out as consultants for the post office and the railroad. As for the Chinese, some of the Kuomintang Republican Chinese posted guards along with the Thais on the border. These KMT were now serving in their third or fourth generation.

Her head swarmed with those who might crawl over the border. Nan leaned forward to catch his soft words.

Mae flared her long, blondish hair in the rare breeze within the compound. She strode toward Ripley and Nan. Bristling, Mae announced, “I'm flying to a base in Vietnam next Thursday. I just got asked to go see the troops. Come on.”

“You're going to entertain the troops?” Nan asked, still wondering if she could travel alone.

"Except for the nabobs, the nobility,” Ripley was saying, “Thais are country folk without hierarchies and with enough Buddhist flexibility to vary their institutions for new overall well-being."

Mae interrupted him. “You're saying the Thais were never conquered.”

“It appears not,” he replied. With his ruddy, fair-haired good looks, Nan thought, he should be called Boone. His outdoor style shouldered a load, and his height was tall, growing taller like a tower, the better to survey the land for forest fires.

“What are you doing here in Thailand?” Mae asked.

“Up North,” he answered, “we're winning some tribes over in their willingness to grow crops that are easier to plant than their opium." He was laughing without explaining. Sneering might follow. Instead, he bent near and almost whispered. “The tribes have been moving south from Laos and China hill to hill, slashing and burning without bother about forests and boundaries. I teach them self-interest. The Meo have really taken to growing pigs. Now they’re family wealth. Just think, these were American pigs only two generations ago. It’s late.” He jumped up. “I’ve got to run. Keep in touch.” He galloped across the grounds into the hostel, evidently to check on someone.

* * *

While waiting for Mae to go back and pick up a hat to wear against the sun, Nan crouched on the ground just outside the gate. They wore their loose blouses, Mae in white and Nan in pale yellow, over black pants and scuffs on their feet.

Four imps were flitting in tag. Nan craned at first to watch them. For several years, she’d studied for degrees in child psych without knowing what exactly she would opt for. Watching these sandy, bare-bottom children, one was always "it." Except when he scampered across the silent line separating the street from the compound. He giggled when she tried grabbing his hand. Someone, an older girl child from a school, perhaps an aide, an older sister, uniformed for a family member, snatched him from the outside pavement.

Meanwhile, within the next compound, young girls in white shirts and dark navy skirts marched out of the side of the L-shaped building, evidently the school side. They lined up for the raising of the Thai flag. They returned to their classrooms.

As for the bare bottoms, their wee tag leader wiggled and unwound himself from his captor, a young woman, a teacher or aide. Giggling, he scrammed to his safety.

Unweaving herself from her class of giants, Nan tried many times standing self-

certain, taller than these tiny boys who slipped away into cottages or shacks. On this edge of the city, a remnant of a fine toy-like village rendered itself now as a city neighborhood. From the corner of the avenue, at her right angle of vision, some better-off Thai homes and cottages had wood stained deep brown or almost cherry. Built tectonic for popular elegance, they mitered contrasting patterns in verticals, diagonals, and horizontals. Some home, inhabitants hung handmade white cut-work curtains over private windows and rolled out royal blue awnings or outside hangings on porches against sun and storminess that would fall on the ribbed terra-cotta roofs. These houses simplified the city. Paralleling the palms along the street and avenue farther on, orderly row of parasols in bright turquoise, red-orange, blood red, and dark blue lined up outside one small home to signify its yard. By contrast, the city wrought its complexity into its great temples.

From her line of vision, from where she stood, she could be anywhere, in any country. Strolling on this avenue, she could be summering in the States. The filling station down the block, the department store, and farther on, a diner in the sameness of this avenue of Thailand to what she knew made travel placeless, ageless, and timeless. As she moved across the land, Indochina, she was suspended, strangely unconfined.

Sauntering out of the compound, Ripley was breathing in the delicacy of her Thai roommate she had caught sight of but not yet spoken with. Nan thought to wave but withheld her hand as too far from them to be seen. At this time, Mae, having deposited her bags, exited the hostel compound. Beneath her wide-brimmed straw hat, her blonde hair bounced with her step beneath her full khaki pants-skirt and bright green Tee. Staying shadowy in the heat, they set out for the market, winding under any shelter, whether awnings or walkways, as much as possible. Nan was anticipating the spices: cumin, lemongrass, and others.

Eventually, the Temple-Place, orange-red and green accented, was sighted. Dragons were flying off the corners of this complex, memorable, immemorial–king-like and fierce in guarding and giving.

That night at the hostel, she met a figurine, her other roommate, a Thai. Whatever this exquisite woman said, it coiled, rolled, or gyrated in Nan's head, trying to rest in some groove or convoluting.

The tiny young Thai spoke accented English. “You like dress woman make me? I buy pretty cloth in Sampeng, where Thais go. See earrings my boyfriend bargain for. Yes, I try to take you there.”

The hostel placed everyone enough in touch to speak. The Thai disclosed a boy as her fiancé. She rolled out two Thai silk, shantung-like with imperfect weaving by design. One, pale ice blue, was stamped with dark blue and rose butterflies and the other gold, offering green and coral flowers rotating around each other.

“Mother want me to marry Thai,” the Thai said. “I say no, so, oh, she mad with me, and we do not speak.

She hates me work. So, I move out, because I want fun. I not mature enough to marry. She say, must I work to be happy? Then work in family busyness with trucks going all over Thailand." The round eyes of the Thai closed. She then smiled, erasing her sadness. Her eyes brightened when she asked, "You have fun here? Go by New Petchaburi Road, where Americans go for fun.

"You know sometime that they feel hostess there is girl friend. Soldiers marry hostesses. Sometimes I go there to seal a deal. Fun. Be careful. Mother mad to see Thai with Westerner.

"Thank you. I learn English in the States in Chicago nine months at business school. Now I sell land in Florida for American Company. Oh, s'cuse me. Bell for me. My boyfriend supposed to call for me. From Chicago but lives everywhere now. He fun to go with to Chieng Mai this weekend. Many flowers there. Go to Chieng Mai and to Sampeng."

Thereafter, the Thai in crystal heels and earrings and eyes laid out photos of her life for Nan who could not figure out who was who. The images backed up in her mind. From where Nan sat the next morning within the compound, she registered only the many apple-like plants, oddly like ones in her Midwest. Again, she waited for Mae or anyone who might cross her path for another Bangkok outing before heading North to see what she could see.

Along came Mae in her floppy straw over her floating hair and dress. Nan tried imitating the throw of Mae's head of hair, but her darker hair would not toss. "What's wrong with your head?" Mae asked.

"Nothing," Nan replied. They set out with guidebooks

for on the cheap. They passed old women whose heads were shaved out of respect for the dead. Boys or men on work crews dressed in royal blue shirts flicked or slapped their scuffs on the pavement.

At once, she spun on her heels. Her eyes skewered five boys at about a three-meter distance behind her and Mae. Asia was growing a breed of youths, haunting the two of them between two points. These would-be layabouts could not find work to do all the time, except at times, when they picked up dirty dishes in restaurants, docked the tourist boats on the Chao Phrya and dove under them to take off weeds on the propellers. Their crew-trimmed heads jutted in sturdiness for hewing. No gentle Buddhas in appearance were they.

Flamboyants, she imagined, magnolia and hibiscus-like flowering trees or hidden bushes perfumed the air, as the boys asked them if they sold themselves. "How much you cost?" The boys signaled by raising a middle finger, as if to give the finger. It was unfair. What had she done except to be where she was? When does a finger become a fist?

* * *

Glancing back and down, she avoided the eyes of those behind Mae and her. Their dusty feet were closing in. Swirling, she tested whether they would follow. "Mae! Cut over to the middle of the avenue by the klong, the canal."

"That one behind us' is no kid," Mae yelled. "Run into the next open compound."

"There aren't any here," Nan replied. She rushed up

to an official-looking man coming toward them and wearing epaulettes. But he knew no English. She thrust here shoulder bag out in back to keep one youth in particular at a distance. "Mae, slow down. Go easy. See if he passes us." Suddenly she hissed and demanded, "See four more."

The one closest to them lit a cigarette. Mae shrieked. "Watch out. He's near you."

Nan yelled and angled her arm to the burn on her back. They dashed through the gate of a stucco building. No one was in the large lounge. She sank on a bench. Mae wet some of her tissues for Nan. While Nan dabbed her wound, she gazed at blow-ups of scaly tumid people exhibited. Some bore open sores with pus or scars, impressing her as victims of catastrophe.

Footsteps began echoing around them from above. A slow walking, marching rhythm billowed around them from a curling stairway. Someone suppressed a laugh. Another coughed. Giggling spurted. Giggles wagged around them into hilarity. Nan felt weak and faint in this cloud of hee-hawing.

She reeled when Mae ordered, "Let's get out of here."

First though, Mae strode over to the laughing eyes, as if to spike them. A man turned toward Nan, then spoke in Thai or Chinese, to a younger man in white. This elder graying man approached the boy who was slouching outside with others against the wall.

Meanwhile, Nan was resting sideways on a stretcher, rolled over from her stomach by a woman in white. Smells and colors were colliding around Nan. The breeze was rippling through the palms, like green knives with serrated edges.

"I sorry." The older man said as he and the woman curved over her. "We cannot get into our first aid room. Clinic closed at this time for the treatment of venereal disease. We're holding a seminar. Wait for our car to return to drive you to where you stay. Or you leave, and we hold that unruly boy out there."

* * *

Nan had assumed she was exempt from the skirmishes of the city. Bangkok spread on and on and was occupied at that time by unnumbered strangers, many in nonclinical khaki. Before leaving it, she noticed Jim Ripley was gunning his motor scooter. He had called out that he was leaving the city for the Northwest.

Taking everyone's advice, she said a temporary good-bye to Mae and tried to trust fate that she would meet another hiker from home or a friend of Mae in a Chieng Mai hostel. Mae was going south. They might meet up again later.

Nan boarded the train North. At times, it unaccountably halted. When sleepy in the fervid heat of the rain forest, she converted the train switches at station stops into rifles that pointed at the sky.

All the same, the train crawled on. A Thai family across from her seat, like a screwed-down wooden bench, gave her a piece of mango. When she smelled it, she hungered for it, though feared the bladder trouble it might cause. Like a puppet, her head strung by a cord though detached from her body, wobbled and bobbed. While managing to stand to stretch, she smiled and bowed to them.

Reaching Chieng Mai, she gaped at the numerous recreation and rehabilitation hotels for American soldiers. They little surprised her, or yes, they did. Outlandishly, they rose bigger, as soldiers lengthened next to Thais in height. She chose a guest house, off-track. Mae was scheduled to catch up to her. If necessary, Nan would move. After her check-in, she settled, the mosquito netting over her the house linen.

She next located an army canteen for meals, until she improved on it with local Thai cuisine. A gussied-up blonde on the bench across the table from her asked, "Want to fly over to the war? It's a quick flight." Nan scrunched her shoulders and flexed them. "Oh." She slurped up welcome mashed potatoes and gravy.

* * *

A cheap trip, she told herself before turning in for the night. Beneath her netting, she tried to scribble in her notebook and sketch. She started, sat up. A dog howled; another whined. She looked out and saw only a full moon and a dim light. A motorbike or other vehicle was gunning. Stilted, she eyed the night scene.

Suddenly, Jim Ripley whizzed off into the night. He was the one whose size she recognized. Her own stomach galloped.

The next day the guest house proprietor lent her a detailed map of the area.

Eventually, she hooked up with three Europeans, hoofing around Chieng Mai.

Their poking around for beer and snacks landed them at dusk within an enclosure in a courtyard. The music rolled and pitched for a lithe, dancing Thai who shimmied and shed her bronze sarong-like wrap-around her pale golden body. Her dancing, like a plume, engrossed her fans. They applauded, hooted, and soft-whistled.

Later, Nan identified this Asian as her former roommate with only the crystal slippers from the Bangkok guest house. Ripley was now here up north at the city-edge Chieng Mai guest house, and strolled over to speak to Nan at breakfast. The former roommate waved to Nan. "She wants me to tell you," Ripley said, "that a girl's family is honored when she's chosen to dance." Shortly thereafter, he and the Thai with the crystals buzzed away on his cycle.

* * *

In the countryside, the tribal members were flowering the hills. Their names like Meo, Karen, and La Hu wore hand-woven dresses with mostly red blooms. It seemed they were floating in the heights. The only way to one of their sacred peaks, Doi Sutep, was to rent the back of a motor scooter, driven by a Thai student in uniform. Nan wound her arms above his waist in unfamiliarity and placed her head on his upper back during the cycle ride that skittered, veered, and edged upward.

Finally, on the mountain, her terrified self eased out her breath. She relaxed and she saw. Just after dawn, the sun gilded the land, during the time of watch and wait. Indochina's peaks with Doi Sutep mounted to form the spine of Asia, stretching around a great ball.

Alabaster New Year

In life, Hasan Ali and Sharin could have come straight out of the *Shahnemah.* Before they arrived at Universal House, they were unseen. Or they could have stepped out of or off the *apadana* of *Takt-e-Jamshid.* Originally located at Persepolis, the Greeks from the West had singed this palatial marble tableau more than the desert could have done in a thousand summers.

They were now upturning it into a veritable table. After searching the crowded great hall place, a newcomer sat down at it with them. At this opening fall dinner, she with her noon hair paused among Iranians and near-Iranians with their midnight hair and Farsi, Persian, and some Arabic.

Next to her, Sharin, her hair sprung off the ledge of her face, gusted with laughter over her work. "I try harmonizing bentwood and womb chairs with Persian carpets."

Across from this tiny artist in interiors and at a diagonal from Anne sat a scientist in earth depths. The tallest at the table, he smiled from some eternal distance.

From his right hand, he could have tossed her a turban scarf. Its meters of iridescence flew the blue-green, maroon and sand brown like colors of his Great Plateau. Reaching her from the Great Plains, the turban unrolled a dream, reopened with fullness and ardor.

* * *

At Universal House, U House, they met. Anyone there could choose anyone else from endless nationalities that sped from around the world, from many worlds. Each was apt to intersect with any other, combining gifts, states of mind, sex, or politics to a point. On their city block, they wove a grid over an orb.

On her first morning at the U House, its aureole dappling, she grew susceptible to possibilities. At her first breakfast, a sidelong shadow stood there. English clouds perhaps faded his skin a few years ago and her's eons ago. She tasted the syrup on her waffle as he half-apologized for waking her so early in the a.m. She waved him welcome. He sat down. She sat up.

Brought up on Gauguin paintings on posters of women in roses, dahlias, flamboyants, and lilies draped on their bodies, she plied her brushes with a palette of the full-color spectrum for her first Tahitian or Fijian. In her world, boys in sailor white forever fancied the full-bodied girls with their leis. Here though, a Pacific Islander unnerved her on the Manhattan island where she lived.

This sun-starred male anthropologist by way of London was setting out to study the first Pacific island nation-state. He could return now that he had just semi-starred in his first feature Hollywood film. Such was one inhabitant, the first met at breakfast at Universal House.

Two weeks later, after the dinner where Anne had met Sharin and Hasan Ali, Anne slipped on the snow, almost landing at the feet of his peak, met coming back from a church bazaar. Upon pulling her up, he smiled out of his dark-eyed scowl, below his wide tawny forehead framed by black hair and cheered, saying, “For five dollars, I found a suit that fit me.”

They strolled on the first snow of the season. Karakal, white lambskin, robed the park. Looking toward an unseen horizon, he told her the snow reminded him of the Zagros mountain land of his youth and in Teheran near North to Demavand, the highest Iranian peak, snow-capped in midsummer against the light azul sky.

At the moment when they climbed the steps to U House, he confided, “I have just published my ninth scientific paper. Others are in the works, what they say. You should come to dinner tomorrow afternoon. At my apartment, celebrate with me. Someday I should be famoose.” His height cloaked over and around her. She backed away. His coat off, the black hairs on his forearms contoured over the muscles that rose with his face in watchfulness. He moved toward her. Warily, she agreed to dinner.

* * *

Back up on her floor in U House, she was about to knock on Sharin’s door, until she heard a low prayer to Allah. A little later, after seeing Anne with Hasan and praying, Sharin had gone to Anne’s door. In her continental boarding school English, Sharin asked, "Do you not think Hasan Ali is one of the kindest of the kind?" Anne smiled.

To that Sharin persisted, “I thought you knew him.”

Anne remembered having seen twentyish Sharin and

Hasan Ali several times ahead of her in the U House dining room line. There he bent over to hear her and speak to her tiny stature. She hippity-hopped around him and dashed out words up to his height with a manner of gravity.

To Anne, she was now saying, "Hasan Ali takes care of everyone, drives everyone everywhere and makes them dinner. He even advises me on my designs. I don't mind, really. But he does furnish his living room with a worn sofa and a hassock from the junk on the street. Of course, he espouses peculiar ideas, like Iran for Iranians, along with his studies of faults. He specializes in the San Andreas Fault, and the one under the River Jordan. He researches what I do not understand."

Here in her U House room, Sharin was voicing over Anne's doubts about agreeing to this dinner. "But he does come from one of our most eminent tribes. And don't you see, he does possess an inferiority complex under a superiority complex. In English, like Farsi, he speaks very much like my parents' servants." She spoke in her boarding school English.

Next, Anne admired Sharin's balsa model of the main floor in her family home back in North Teheran. To redecorate the miniature, she reconstructed its entrance with a small, stair-sized ziggurat that she marbleized. On one side, she duplicated its family dining room and on the other its great hall for great events.

The next day Hasan Ali was dressed in a blue flannel shirt above his black cords, baggy at the knees, when he welcomed Anne at his apartment house six doors down from U House, where he had lived there for two years. His living room was chance, as described by Sharin.

From it, he led her into the kitchen and sat her down next to Davud who smirked slightly when Hasan Ali introduced her.

A wedge within her pushed her to go back to U House to study and hide. Uneasy at first, she stayed.

"I don't know how," Hasan Ali was saying, "how this meal will turn out, because Davud and I cook with our noses." A meal already fixed did away with her wish for escape.

"Anne," he, his eyes a-wink, appealed to her in a break from stirring his sauce. "Your name sounds like our word for prostitute in Persian." Appalled, she sat there. "You could be for us American Grace or Spanish Linda or any other name." Still she sat. For the time being she cast off her name. Nothing else mattered other than getting through the meal. After trying out names—Lily, Violet, Terry, Flo, Liz, Chloe, Mallory—she chose Grace.

"Grace," Davud beckoned her to the other side of the stove to see the tunnels in the cooked rice, intimacies of a shared household she was wary of and drawn to. He lifted off the crust and identified it, "the best part of the rice."

During the meal, Hasan pressed her, "Eat more *dolmeh, pilaf, khoeshte fesenjan* with pomegranate. Next time, I make shish kebab you expect." Obliged to eat until overfilled and vexed, she ate only shavings of green baklava for dessert. She imagined herself fattening up to suit some Middle Eastern style of female body, though the ones she saw at Universal House were slender.

"In our house," he proclaimed, "to get attention, we never stopped eating until our guests did." As for Grace, she chewed no more and swallowed.

"Ours too!" Davud, a short, compact man with a round face, slowed his speech and squinted his already narrow eyes. "I would think twice before inviting you, Hasan Ali. You're a human garbage disposal, you eat so much."

"When your girlfriend moved out," Hasan retorted. "She left her Afghan to take up leftovers you waste."

He was more pleased with Davud's mother's baklava than his remark admitted. Between bites, he drank glass after glass of tea from his dented samovar he had found in a thrift shop. Upon swallowing, his body seemed to verge on swelling, overflowing like an open *qanat*, a human-made underground rivulet to water the land and clean the city. Because of her public health field, this watering system intrigued her. She watched this human *qanat*, as Davud designated him with barbs.

Thumping back onto the chair's hind legs, Hasan sat arms on the armrests and relished his well-being.

"Your father," he said to Davud, "was lucky to get such a woman who sends you, her son, forty pounds of pistachio, this baklava, and a hand-knit sweater to keep you warm."

Anne-Grace listened, ruminated on how some woman could be lucky to win such a man like Hassan, who could offer such a meal as his. Satisfied, she was trying to overcome her habitual post-dinner sleepiness and her doubts. Could she win him and a career too? She sipped her tea and forgot to ask for lemon.

"Yes, my father lost his fortune with bankruptcy." Davud said and switched into Farsi with Hasan Ali.

In each century, Hasan Ali had sailed farther west in

each century. A new town was built, displacing a tribe here, housing a tribe there. He, Hasan, migrated with his family inward to new settlements and onward.

* * *

Later, Hasan Ali and Anne-Grace entered his room, as if into a magi-made kiosk to look out of. On the floor lay the deep red Bakhtiari carpet, a lozenge with arabesques within three borders. On one long side, huge posters swept up her eyes from west to east. He seemed to apologize for having no poster of Najaf shrine of Ali. Ah, but to see Esfahan was to be spirited away to enchantment. Esfahan lay to the south of the east to west line as the Florence or Kyoto of Iran. There, in Esfahan, blue calligraphy, geometry and arabesques were webbing the inner dome of the madrassah. In another of his big wall posters, greenery spread over an unknown Paradise, bred from the desert.

In the third poster, the Mosque of the Last Imam at Meshed signified the reign of the hidden Twelfth Imam that wafted down through contemporary time for Hasan and Grace. Decembers back and away, the twelve were finalizing in Hussein. He resounded to Grace, familiarized by her messiah and his twelve, and his sometime return as Mahdi someday.

Below Hasan's posters, a plain dresser and one twin bed stood. On the end of the white room opposite the door, a glass wall, ceiling to floor, the palisades sky-scraped the clouds.

Metal bookcases ran the length of the other long wall, where Grace probed for talk from among his books in winged script. Most she found in English on political theory, Physics, Geophysics, and Oceanography. While she floated and scanned the volumes, Hasan Ali let go from soft and striking memory poetry of Rumi, Hafiz, and Ferdowsi from his *Shahnameh*, Sa'adi—some of their lines in Farsi and some in easygoing English from time to time for her. Also, he spun out Sufi ecstasy.

When she slipped from his trance and lore to gaze out the window, he seemed unaware. There were oil drums labeled with the name, though not the family, of the man she was unsure she ought to have left not long before. Nevertheless, she relaxed back on the carpet, plush in deep red and blue, the only comfort other than the light blue chenille of his bedspread, where he lay blazed in the late day sun.

From squinting out the window, as his rounded oblong face rolled toward hers, the darks of his eyes were enlarging to shade and observing her. He extended his arms across the mile to hers where she sat. His hand cushioned hers, but she leaned back on her elbows and inquired, "Just where do you come from?"

His road was lying at the same latitude as hers; only hers existed at a diagonal through the earth. On his road, personal growth followed prehistory. Women in turbans and men in skullcaps among his people had been pasturing their animals from place to place across the Zagros, their three rivers into an estuary, seaming back to the earliest Persians. His Bakhtieri rode horseback north of the Turkic Qashqai and the Arabians, lumbering across the desert cinnamon.

Away from its storms, his family's clayey brick abode was lined with lime against the wind. Inside his family circled and sat around their fire. It was set into a meter-wide ground vessel to warm themselves asleep or awake, as he and his brothers and sisters were growing up. His father would decide, he said, whether to leave to cross the sands with the rest of the family that would follow in due time.

"We sat in front of our red brick fireplace," she whispered back to him, so as not to intrude. "On Sundays, my parents and sister ate supper there, but they stayed in one place."

He continued that while his father was arranging their way to reach the capital, his mother, enthusiastic about advancing her family, placed him and his younger sister in a half-circle around their schoolmaster.

In that old mid-century, some great unknown or misunderstood dynamism was looming. Like their more enterprising kin who dwelled where oil was discovered during the Great War somewhere far away, she later urged her son to become "a doctor in oil, black gold."

When his father sent for them from Tehran, the life shift began. His grandfather sat him on a burro and mother and sister on a donkey and he on another. They rode out across the desert to stop at a caravanserai for the night. One day, he at age six fell sideways while on the burro. His lopsidedness unnoticed until they reached the Esfahan bus stop, he could not adjust himself, but he did not cry.

"The only beast of burden," Grace interjected, "I, a tiny girl, ever rode was neither a donkey nor burro. Only the old Chevie I rode in lurched and wiggled, so I fell between the front seats."

Broadly speaking, her family from Europe did the

same as his from Europe. With each set of grandparents, her family founded and moved from gristmill to gristmill, until her grandfather owned land. Only after he sold it, oil spurted there. But she only became a Master of Public Health and soon, hopefully, Hasan Ali a Doctor of oil.

Upon coming here, before delving into his geophysical doctorate, Hasan studied two subjects. He professed to comprehend neither English women nor American women well. Grace leaned toward him to listen to his soft, deep speech.

"I tell truth." He wagged his head. "Back home, I sleep on the roof in summer with family. I looked on cousin on my uncle's roof next door.

"When I come here, to America, at first, my best friend nun." Her black habit recalled women at home in cheddar. Their habits, Grace thought, made mountains out of women. Yet in due time, his mother and sisters wore them sometimes outdoors, not indoors. Substance, not shadow, Grace believed, presence, not absence. The nun guided Hasan in English, till he could find synonyms on his own. Another, a wife of a town mayor, taught him colloquialisms. So, Grace gleaned that Hasan Ali might collect more than words.

"For seven years, my cousin has been waiting for me," he commented. Grace asked her age then. "Since she was fourteen." Grace, then, slipped and told him about the man whose name was on the oil drums across the river. Dryly, Hasan observed, "Oil keeps coming up for a while."

In Iran, she decided, scientists speak in poetics to lure, though this one's bed fit only one person. From Sharin and her friends, two women could lie parallel to each other even on a single bed in U House, a divan or carpet, or supposedly two men. But a man and a woman?

Outside the deep azure came up with the stars. "You can stay," he announced.

"I have calculations to do."

"You do. You have been calculating all along."

"Work, I mean, statistics."

"Everyone does. That is how I spend my spare time."

She left abruptly.

* * *

Grace knocked on the door. Sharin answered and offered her some pilaf, kosher from a deli. Her Islamic orthodox diet as practiced then resembled the Jewish diet. Sharin, jovial from her tasty dish and whatever else, asked. "Grace, are you going with Hasan Ali to Washington? He told Zal who told Ali who told Tauriq who told me."

In those days, Grace denied this trip to protect Sharin from over-exposure to the world. "Never mind. Tauriq from Turkey," Sharin owned up, "pursues me to go with him." Next to this petite one poised with her floss of hair and silk shirt the exact color of her turquoise ring, Anne-Grace felt slipshod and wrinkled in jeans and a jersey. Sharin frowned. "But in my dreams, my grandfather tells me to reject this offer."

"Tell me, will you marry Hasan?" Sharin asked. Grace jerked up and protected herself through denial.

"In that case, Marcia is good for him," she emphasized, "big like him. Big women and her field—poli sci—please him. They have been planning to marry."

Anne, feeling skinny and undernourished, listened. The tall woman had promenaded with Hasan Ali the summer before last, when Anne had visited U House. His memorable size and face first impressed her.

Alas, she, Grace-Anne, saw herself entering a contemporary tie of the Indo-Aryan-European sixth form of marriage between the unmarried. She and Hasan swept up each other and warmed, billowed and writhed like the mounting sands of the desert. And rested on their sides, facing each other, like two lengthy plateaus.

Sharin was bubbling that Marcia appreciated Hasan's politics and studies. At this time, he researched the earth's upheavals, rather than those of the world, as Marcia did. He no longer debated his fellow students. Because of his wariness, Sharin marked him as a higher male and added. "I hate crude politics."

"But Hasan also loves music and poetry," she added, "and the old Charles Aznavour records we listened to last *Nawruz*." Instantly, she asked, "Are you sure you do not want to marry Hasan?"

To Grace's smile and shrug, Sharin replied, "If not, then maybe I will introduce him to my cousin, who is beautiful, tall, and clever enough for him."

"He is always saying that the Iranian government and circumstance are demanding he go back to our country. Because of all his governmental fellowships, he must go or face loss of respect."

* * *

That night, some urgency propelled Hasan to visit Grace in her twin-sized bed for the first time. Usually, they had stayed in his. His ribs muscled his skin, contoured by his hairy over-brush, bushy on his chest, smooth to her touch. Rather than sleep or rest and dream, after lovemaking they whispered.

Afterward, he enjoined her to understand that he and Davud had been arguing over Davud's share of the cooking for others in their circle and Hasan's carting them around to one party or many meetings, including prayer, Davud attended and Hasan was seeking to avoid. Their circle of Iranian friends credited Hasan, yes, he said so, for his activity on their behalf, though he seldom now went along to their get-togethers.

Huffily and abruptly, Davud had moved out from Hasan's place that day and in again with his girlfriend. So, Hasan thought, the former girlfriend of Davud, it turned out, was missing her Afghan. So, with this large animal with the fur that was flying, Davud was moving into her apartment, larger than that of Hasan. The exit of his friend bothered Hasan.

Moreover, Hasan was piqued. The journal editor of his latest article left off his, Hasan's name, on his twelfth-to-be published paper.

So, he welcomed Grace on the same pillow as his. Or she him on hers, though he had brought his own to her twin bed. She had long invited him to her pillow. When there, he cooed, "Come live with me in my place."

Overwhelmed, she leaned back on her elbow. The candle was flickering. She asked back to his asking, taunting. "Why not marry Marcia?"

"Really, I am very sentimental. When I called you earlier, your voice sounded just like hers. But Marcia is married now and living in Omaha."

"Then too," Grace reminded him, "you've been engaged for years. You told me so yourself."

"I am worth waiting for." His head, above her on his pillow, tipped from side to side.

"You never tell me these things."

"I have, to Sharin."

"She matters?"

"She has indicated her interest. Her size is too tiny for me."

"And your cousin?"

"My cousin studies business in the West and Midwest."

"No wonder you study the San Andreas fault!" She was, she told herself, spiking any interest in herself.

"You in your country," Hasan Ali said, as if he were not here, "are all alike. You are thinking about our same-time marriages. But you have more than we dream about." By now, he released himself from the bed, reached for her desk chair and sat with his legs around its back, facing her while leaning his arms on it. "You have been ruining life for everyone everywhere else. You Americans with all your machines are romantics—always looking for one and only one to love and your best device. You keep changing which one.

"Only, there is no one and only." He smiled from his perch. "Never mind about machines. Many wives or husbands save you from loneliness."

"You wanted to hear that, didn't you? How about wife confidante and consultant?"

Cousins, cousins, Grace thought and said so.

Hasan Ali responded. "You be my cousin, if you want. You move back in with me and stay." She smiled. Until the removal of her wisdom teeth, she had been staying with him. Now, having recovered from their removal, she was back in her place.

In that time with him, he gave her the turban scarf, a runner that unwound from around her head or his floor to floor. It was, he told her later, just what a Dr. Molsefedeh, an obstetrician friend of his, ordered him to give Grace for her recovery.

In these days, unlike Grace's melancholy, Hasan's cheer came from another source, other than her. A university had invited him to be a visiting full professor.

* * *

One evening, months later, before going to the Spanish dance party at U House, they ate a meal at a nearby grill. While talking about next to nothing, he was eyeing a woman at the next table. She filled an electric blue blouse, and her hair was midnight. Grace overheard her speaking with a third man in an unknown tongue. When he was paying the cashier in the front, and Grace was returning from the toilet, the electric blue blouse was handing a note to Hasan Ali.

Outside he and Anne-Grace walked along the riverbank. The warming atmosphere under the scarlet sun against the navy brooding sky was thawing the river and cracking its iced surface to make a boom of chunks that whooshed down to the ocean. Lower in their view of the distance, beneath the tangle of stars, the bridge linked some into a string of crystals that Hasan broke. "Oh, I feel young again. That was a tasty meal."

A couple of male passers-by stared at Grace-Anne.

She glared back.

Hasan announced to her, "Whatever you do away from me, do not tell me."

"But I have nothing to tell you or keep from you."

"What about oil drum name over there?"

"He never came back."

After they circled back to U House, Hasan argued with a political science woman student. He labeled her "naïve."

A mathematician greeted Anne-Grace. Frequently they rode together on the elevator of their wing though to different floors. At the Spanish dance, he asked her to dance. Dance she did.

Moments thereafter, his meal no longer cheered Hasan. Nor was he his usual bobbing peak on the dance floor. Usually he loved to dance.

His exterior was tightening into a cord of fibers around a steely center, glowing and dimming. "We are a couple! Everyone thinks so. All the Persians do. Do not," he began to say, directing her to the hall, to the front door, down the sidewalk, to his front door, to his apartment door in the same block as U House. "Do not dance with that fellow. A year ago, Davud drove him to the airport. The next he knew authorities were interrogating him."

Anne-Grace wondered if Hasan Ali objected to the mathematics of their quandary. Or was the problem one value of his theory or the country of the man to the North of his?

Hours later, on a June night, back in his apartment, Hasan snatched an air letter from his table his brother had written him. The research money Hasan gathered helped support the younger one. Now his brother was insisting that he needed more. Of necessity, he had married a French anthropology student. "For all the years," Hasan Ali intoned this. "My father struck me as a child and never paid for school for me; I was scholar in family. He counted on me to pay for my young brothers. One better turn out doctor." The blacks of Hasan's eyes fired and darkened.

Grace slanted her eyes at the bookshelf: Creep, Creep Structure, and Earth and Physics. Opening one at random she spotted a note about the stable shelf beneath the unstable one. Minutes later he put his pillow fingers on her neck. She backed off and said, "I am going home."

"You are home; I am not home." He recited Rumi.

"You have not seen me for the last three Saturday nights."

"After our yearly laboratory picnic, I saw you last Saturday night." His voice cracked. She countered that he had not. After a ride back with colleagues of his, she had returned to her place.

On the last, most recent Saturday, a daytime lab get-together had occurred. At his institute, his would-be *madrassah*, his charts, world maps, and his printouts of earthquake patterns were pinned up around the mainframe. Yet he was working from his new, small laptop computer. Didn't he remember?

From his white-walled office with carpeted floor, she had set off on that day to go to sit on a rock and work on her own. En route, she had slipped down an incline, landing by a huge box, lettered, "Do not open without permission." Suddenly, guards surrounded her and asked her to leave, until she identified herself as a guest of Hasan. Told about the incident, he had humored her as, "my top secret."

Back here and now, she reminded him of her view. "You drove me home."

"I don't like to go out on Saturday night, the most hectic night of the week. Then, I work here or there with computer, in quiet lab."

"As men go, you are awfully independent," she noted.

"You Americans are very independent; you go off by yourself and you want your identity. But you complain of loneliness. It is true, I depend only on myself." He leaped up to shower in his bathroom.

Anne was sinking on one of Sharin's finds, a bentwood chair Sharin had bought second-hand months earlier and handed to Hasan. Even so, he chided her on wasting wood, burned or used up, their land sun-scoped, stark and dramatic. She had tut-tutted, imitated him, and giggled. Anne now wished Sharin to be here in his living room, rather than far at home.

Minutes later in a robe, he reentered. His hair damp on his body, he slumped on his divan, his feet one on it and one on his lumpy couch.

She was uneasy and walked toward the door.

"Wait," he ordered her. "I am not ready to give you up. You never bore me." She turned back to see him and walked toward him. His eyes were veined. He said, "I am always alone."

* * *

Like the Afghan, Hasan was awaiting his new home with eyes closed within his dark brown face and long, furry, light brown outer hair and was jump-ready from under the table. Anne-Grace was alerting herself to the future. Warm and damp, Hasan came out again of his shower. He loved showers. They hugged.

Davud, having moved away into a new apartment, was coming for supper and for extra things he'd left behind until he'd changed the locks on the new door of his and his girlfriend's place. Hasan was cooking again for the three of them or four, counting the dog, whoever showed up.

Davud would curb the uneasiness between Grace and Hasan, she thought, because he and Hasan were reconciling, now that they lived apart. They gabbed about his gathering up secondhand furniture. Grace began hearing the "eh" at word endings, as they spoke, in mid-tone and minor key.

Somehow, as Davud was laboring to set up house on his own without any household help, he resumed English on how he and his brothers and sisters grew up with nurses. The oldest nurse was given to his great-grandmother. His family had wanted the nurse to be operated on because of her venereal disease. At that, Grace-Anne threw open her eyelids and groaned in public health virtue.

"That should be very dangerous for your family," Hasan Ali commented to Davud.

"She was cautious and washed a lot," Davud qualified. "She was very kind to all of us. My mother tried to pay her for her work. But this nurse refused by saying a roof overhead was all she needed." He pointed out that she looked like an African black, like ones in their area of New York, now their front door. Only her Persian-ness, he maintained, was visible, though her skin was dark brown and hair white, her appearance born in slavery. "

You cannot wash that away," declared Hasan. Again, he thumped his chair back square onto the parquet. He reached for her glass and poured her more tea. Then, he pished. "No Africans live in Iran."

"You never noticed them; they're almost everywhere." Davud countered. "I know, because of one in our house, and I have seen others in other houses."

"But Sharin says the servants in her house are light-skinned, more Slavic or Turkish."

"Sharin would," Davud replied. He paused. "Another thing, my grandmother served others in a different way. When she grew older, she became more and more known for her formula to help old men. They came from afar to receive her rare compounds."

"Where is Afar?" To this from Grace and her puzzled look, Hasan pooh-poohed his remark. "You too young to know about Spanish fly." Before she could reply that he was too, he reverted to Farsi. She guessed them to be in Iran by their words, until they spoke English again.

"My grandmother," Davud slid back into English for Grace, "could also recite the Koran from cover to cover."

"Mine too!" Hasan Ali saluted grandmothers with another glass cup of tea held high.

Neither of hers, Grace noted, copied that ability, other than recite verses here and there from the Bible.

The paternal grandmother of Davud, he continued, could not read or write. If he covered a page, except for a few words, she could follow up with the whole passage. If he or another picked a random page, she could recite it all by heart.

Ten years after the period, he had done so and later, when Davud left Iran, his father handed him the one book that had belonged to his grandmother. Sacred twice over, her Koran had belonged to her husband and saved him from an assassin's bullet; he'd preserved its hole.

Nodding over their grandmothers, Hasan and Davud slipped back into Farsi and its Iran.

Intrigued by these ancient women, African-Iranian, Slavic, Iranian, Grace requested more data. Both Davud and Hasan jumped up to retrieve it. With reverence, Davud handed her the Koran to study. She poked her finger through the hole in its leather cover with arabesques, turned the pages like onion skin and handed it back.

From Hasan Ali, Grace examined his photo album. In one, a dark boy with a high forehead sat surrounded by women on a carpet. In another, Hasan the young man, face black-mustached and light-bearded, and hair crested, loomed above other family men before he departed for the United States.

Three months later, Anne-Grace herself moved from her first apartment into another several blocks away from the first and from U House. Artie, its superintendent, helped her move in without Hasan.

Meanwhile, Sharin, giddy with news gleaned at home, whispered first distress, "Davud's lost." Anne asked for details, but Sharin knew little.

"Now I introduce you to a cousin, no not mine, but Hasan's. Like his sisters, once young bank clerks, she rose to supervise and, then, study at a Midwestern college."

It came to pass that Sharin next announced to Anne

that Hasan would marry Dr. Molsefedeh, a friend of the Armenian woman bloused in the electric blue. Just as well, Anne decided, for Hasan had long preferred to be a Doctor of Medicine, not of oil.

Thereupon, Anne packed away the turban scarf he'd claimed matched her flickering blue-brown eyes. That was that.

* * *

Not only that, a month later, Anne gazed upon his cousin with Sharin, who was gesturing in the great hall of U House. She chattered on about her projects of redesigning insides of palaces, until the cousin scooted over. "Yes, yes, I am the only child, who grew up next-door to Hasan."

Unlike Sharin's coif, Shala's puffed out as she emphasized all her words. "My cousins spread out. My cousins started in the bank. The men cousins now specialize in oil, anthropology, stones, and carpets. I'm to be stockbroker; I stay here, open own firm."

The U House crystals dangled overhead. Their intricate chandelier pitched them down on Anne, seemingly. The thought flew into her to study a South Pacific atoll, its public health.

After that, by accident she ran into Hasan and congratulated him on his forthcoming marriage. Taking her hand in his, he asked her if he could give her anything. No, she answered, she would preserve the turban scarf, scroll it and unscroll it. All she wished for was to shake his hand for good fortune. "You go to the Middle East; I go to the Midwest." They chuckled. She began to stand aside.

On his shoulder, he had hoisted a metal file box, unlettered, for his research on the continental divide. After that immediate study was concluded, he would journey back to his land of exquisite pieces fit into mosaics, prayers more often than meals, and shadows in habits.

Rescue

"Oh, for a daughter so compliant my limits would not fail to help me. Why didn't I plug Eliza into a system?"

"Thank heavens, El will study horses Anywhere and Dan, in Elsewhere."

Joanna, portly in a maroon dress, twisted her graying ponytail, billowing around her puffy eyes. "You hug her. Then, you lose her."

"Do women ever lock up daughters?" With a grown daughter and son at ten, Paula knew not.

Jo shrugged. In college, she could say anything to Bill. They married, he fell ill. Dying, he asked Jo to keep the girls away from his hospitalized monster-self, hooked to tubes and memories.

"In loving someone, you carry his style with spirit. On his birthday, we two sipped wine through a straw. Next, he died."

* * *

Faithfully, Jo and her daughters stayed near their academy that instilled faith, pride, and safety. From their building threshold across from park palisades, she bemoaned to Paula.

"'The other side of Broadway,' here, kids affect kids more than grown-ups do or does." Across the rocks above Broadway, not sponge, "Eliza, a wild kid, could experiment within discipline for life." Here rain floods gutters, softening ground.

In childhood, Joanna had squished her feet on Florida ocean-shore sand. Now beneath her apartment building sub-cellar, water was seeping into wall cracks from the nearby estuary. Her neighbor-friend, Paula, was planning to escape the city problem with a move to Florida.

"You and your husband," Jo sighed and said, "will select the trusty neighborhood for your son. I'm too easygoing to do so."

* * *

Up in the White Mountains, her relatives thrived in clapboard houses. After her lawyer father died, her mother clicked back into New York. With Jo and her sister, eleven and six, in school, her mother became a Lord & Taylor buyer.

Up "rutsy streets," they moved to a building with iron benches. Above them, only earlier cartoon designs remained of stained-glass windows, looted or sold off by the landlord. Their plum and vermilion outlined figures survived El Greco-like, bent within their frames.

* * *

"First comes beauty, then, the sadness." Upstairs in her place, Jo was clutching the railing into her sunken living room. She lamented, "Mama's suffering. I want her to go out with a 'bromide cocktail.'"

"Drink in your grandmother's wisdom again at the end of her life," she counseled her daughters.

Eliza pleaded, "Can I stay with her?"

* * *

After El's hospital visit to her grandmother, Jo's mother cheered up. "Get me a wheelchair. Let's check out the men. Life's good. I like one. His wife won't mind. I'm dying."

Jo stayed on in the neighborhood of her mother, where her friendliness might get her welcomed into the apartments of her neighbors of every background. Her geniality could also get her attacked in her off-Broadway alleyway. Only firestorms, she brooded, connected all strangers.

To the pounding one day on her apartment door, Jo hooted, "Who's there?"

A neighbor known as Guy, handsome with one long, dark eyebrow, cranked out, "Through the ceiling, your music's driving my father crazy."

Rae, her youngest, played hip-hop and techno. Jo figured out the beats must bother the older man on the floor below.

"And knock off your stomping on the floor," Guy threatened. "Or we will knock you."

"I pace." She half-whispered.

Guy doubted what Jo said. Paula believed him psychopathic.

A few days later, Guy's old man thumped on Jo's door. "Guy'll get you!"

Guy started following El with her new boyfriend. Red-haired Dan's six feet plus, golf irons, and hammers protected her.

Jo searched for crime victims-to-be counseling. “Flee Guy and his Ballbusters,” the precinct captain urged her. She tried warning El about, “gorgeous dudes with teak skin and lacquered duds and red-haired firebrands.”

At 16, long brown gloss-hair a-swinging, she retorted, "Why? Crawl to a decent neighborhood or be friendly with who's here. You always told me so." Off to her Academy, she slammed the door.

Jo confided to her neighbor. "With those ultramarine eyes, El possesses loyalty to Dan. The Ballbusters kicked off his gang." His mother's miscarriages crazed her, riled her husband's war memories and led her to mouth off to her son. Jo tried to interrupt to her daughter, Eliza, to explain the situation. “Guy tried pushing El under a train and threatening Dan. Remember?”

Jo stormed. "Endanger your life. Not mine or Rae’s."

El begged. "Mommy, do rehab with him. Help him."

Penniless, he rode with Jo to their city councilor for aid. Jo aimed for justice, not charity. “Humans go wrong. They can redeem themselves.”

In due time, Jo pegged Dan for college upstate. He thwarted it. "Construction engineering won't admit me. Why bother?"

Taking other credits and waiting a semester up there for his chosen field daunted him. A toothache also became an earache. Owing thousands in tuition, he threatened the loan officer.

The administration next ordered Dan off college grounds. By paying early alum dues, he believed he could win acceptance. Only he wound up hitchhiking back downstate.

* * *

Ambling into their diner many hours later, he sat by Jo. "My late husband would have said to you, 'When you're down, tighten your belt. When you're up, eat.'" Dan ate three hamburgers.

El blurted out, "I'm going to Oklahoma College."

"The first cowboy I find you with I'll shoot," Dan exploded. Moreover, the gang had cell-phoned Guy that Dan was back in the city. Guy stomped in and sneered. "Scum, fight me. Or, I make out with El. Or your mother."

Dan rose. Guy swung. Dan's glasses hit the floor. Punches gusted and whacked Dan. A window cracked. A door was unhinged.

* * *

Two days later, El asked, "Why?" when Dan, bandaged, opposed college.

"No."

Jo half-whimpered to her friend Paula. "El wanted Dan to fix his tooth and shake off Guy."

Dan declared he loved El. His mother would buy her a ring. His first girl dropped him. His loss festered in him. Now he named El, "My Woman."

* * *

The agency victims-to-be group advised Jo to stand with Eliza. How? Jo's only family, never close, evaded her. Her brother-in-law kept her sister away from Jo. Their White Mountain cousin, mustached and big-shouldered, who'd commanded a platoon, grilled her. "Why abandon your daughter?"

* * *

"Physical strength never protected us," Jo confided next to Paula. "Eliza fawns over every male. Loyalty under stress. Someone tell me what to do. I'm the softie. El sees nothing wrong in what she does."

Eliza could "camp" in Oklahoma forever. El tried to humor Dan. Jo prayed for a ploy or a miracle to deal with this situation. "Elisaheva is smitten with Dan whose gang is attacked by Guy's gang. He lives with his father downstairs below El and her two teen daughters. His father grumps about noisy music and clomps overhead. On behalf of his father, he'd threatened El."

* * *

"Let's start a program for violent people?" Jo favored. Dan refused.

"We never do all we believe in," she commented to her friend Paula.

The night before El departed for college in Oklahoma, Jo got a beef sandwich into her and embraced El. They both held Dan. If they walked inside, they tiptoed, so as not to disturb the floor below. Guy was beginning to study for his high school equivalency and college entrance.

Once El reached college, Jo wrote her: "I cannot live

with myself. Strange, your psychologist father, lawyer grandfather, buyer grandmother emboldened themselves. You reincarnate their wills. A daughter is all her best ancestry, with the worst.

"Living on that rock, Eliza, you would never have confronted that your sister and me, who love you, wished to drive you away."

"We're staying, not moving to Florida after all." Paula told Jo a few days later.

“Flat out, my ten-year-old flat out won’t go."

Jo pined, "Do we help each other in life, or only hold each other’s hand?"

Gambe

Can an annual plant crop up again? She did not know. This year Cait would resume and expand her annual supper beyond her cousins, who'd moved away anyway, to some known, especially Polly and maybe Jo with more troubles than her own and semi-known individuals, such as men. She would honor someone to win them into coming to her party.

To honor the birthday of a mutual acquaintance, the first couple to arrive rang and knocked at the open door. They yoo-hooed. No one could answer the door, as her spouse used to do so. Cait was running to dust here and there and straighten soft paper napkins and silverware, actually steel. She'd taught her five- and seven-year-olds to lay the table and fan out the spoons and forks on the dining table's white tablecloth.

As she raced around, it was just about time on her grandmother's cuckoo clock. This twosome entered, jostled by some later arrivals behind in the small entryway. At the doorway, the two women each pecked the others' cheeks.

Ian and Cait, the party-giver, slipped their mutual kisses onto the sides of their necks, by mistake. His wound up on her shoulder, and hers slid beyond his bushy, pale auburn beard below his right earlobe over and down his carotid.

She worried she'd drooled somehow, for in the past,

they'd shaken hands or was it shook, in a good solid grip. Gradually he'd been saying, as he had on the phone and did this time, "Caitlin! It's time we saw you again." Words grew into hugs that gave way to....

Through the years, her mother had always embraced everyone, relatives, school chums, buddies, friends, and their husbands, and kissed them. Cait could not imagine not doing so while hosting. Now without all of them, her mother, her father, her spouse since them, years having passed and a new era having reached her, the puzzle arose whether to hang back and clutch or go it alone.

At her own party, she could hardly formulate her approach. Of the second couple in at the door, Erika had sheared off most of her white-blonde hair except for a tuft on her head top. Jose with his black almost-flattop, gray-flecked, and a goatee, swooped up Cait and presented Erika with great good glee.

At that moment from next-door, her two curly topped towheads dashed in through or around the legs of this tallish couple and down the hallway, deep into the apartment. The partygoers ambled on into the chirping *coquets*, one yellow and the other chartreuse, cockatoos or *coquets* who were cooped in a cage

* * *

As for the grown-ups, he and Cait had run again into each other at a recent specialty conference. They'd rattled on about where they'd been, since they'd last met on a medical study. He'd worked his way up through medical school, first in Santo Domingo, halted to earn more to finish in Mexico, preferred for its cardiologists, rather than its public health specialists. After the recent conference, these conferees let the subject matter bowl them back to his Victorian house. There he entertained her at his kitchen table until she could catch the next train back to the city, according to the RR timetable.

Half-Mexicano and half-Puertoriqueno, Luis had gone from the southern border over to the northern. His technical wife, a non-Latina, Ellen, remained upstairs. He divulged that he lived downstairs because they had fulfilled their time together.

That was the way Cait looked at the end of their marriage and now her own, as best she could. Luis had glimpsed the departure of his wife when she reduced the size of her nose. Or he was leaving—never clear—her. But Cait really cared when her spouse left. There and then, she and the Latino were buddies and talked about what consumed him, his Free, nicknamed Erika.

"Freya would never kiss me or anyone in public," he announced to Cait with a plea for her to clarify or understand. Some Norse code, he thought, must have got set up in North America, at the other, northern border, he restated, near the International Divide.

Cait objected. Not so geographically distant from the same divide, her mother's friends thrived on public hugs. His friend, though, preserved some scruple against private ones. At any rate, their talk across borders had lagged and hung there when her train carried her off.

Their talk came to mind when the other couple, Ian and his Candace, not quite her real name, skipped in. The value of greetings intensified with them and resumed with Freya and Luis at her doorway.

Anyway, at her event, Cait planned to slough off her

woes. Sloth, restlessness, and cravenness popped into her head to stymie her at times. Then and there, her wee duo slipped up and passed them out the door. Out of all the possibilities for Cait, only one folded in her—anxiety.

Only three or four times Cait had met the first couple, the English-y one from the Commonwealth. After the slipped kiss with him, she spotted the boots of the woman, his wife. Supple and fine, their amber matched her slightly darker skin and the deeper red beard of her spouse.

Their skin color blended, their garb did otherwise. Her Saville suit coordinated with her hedge hair trim. His Harris tweed bunched and stretched to contrast with his high-blown coronet of reddish verging on gray, speckling his red beard.

Cait, the party-giver, knew she'd observed this discussant before. He elicited the nuances of some research, as if on the danger of naphtha. Also, she discovered their mutual friend Luis at the same conference. Ian himself presented a public health monograph on some nuance of "loose motions," as the Brits on holiday would call diarrhea. It was apt to be deadly. Automatically public health doctors, such as Luis, Candace, and Ian, knew this problem as the number one killer in the developing world. From covering it for a newspaper for internists, Cait planned on handing over Candace's own introductory speech on this problem to her.

Afterward, days later, Ian requested the copy Cait already promised to her. She'd forgotten and justified her failure to herself as, "a divorce that consumed me."

The name of his wife, Candace, was biblical. Whether

her given name or an Ethiopian one added onto her from their time in East African, Cait was puzzled. Actually West African, Candace, slender and erect, modeled a special self in contrast to the self of her Scots-English husband.

His body burly and his hairy face, disguised his expressive mouth too much to tell whether he was puckish or serious, as his eyes stared at Cait. She wished she'd stayed secretive to evade his being seductive. From his speech, she uttered, "serious?" Seer? He bluffed. Sure.

In her, then, cold sickliness stole into her. She recalled the case he presented. An imprisoned husband and wife were each sick. With what was it? Lousy motions or trauma, neither of which she ever suffered from.

Instead of thinking, she would enjoy her party. Besides, it seemed to be perking along for the moment. She jacked up the sound of Muddy Waters.

Oh, yes, now she remembered what Ian said. At his seminar, he concluded, "One needs to share one's feeling life with someone." She tried to dismiss his words. At such gatherings for advanced medical learning, where she heard him, doctors made their names in trial runs for journals. They reserved speech for upholding new ideas. She'd strained on that time, as he spoke, to sit still. But wished to fly away. Why did his words wound her? No time to figure it out. Race to the restroom stall. Sob about the end of her marriage—so commonplace no one else could relate to it as significant.

* * *

Her dinner or supper could pull her out of her doldrums. Recently her father sat down one day and died in early old age. Next her spouse stood up and left. Inside and out, she ordered herself to give this party. Her apartment building's master custodian, Artie, replaced the worn-out connector tube between her old dishwasher and the sink and slammed a window she could not reach for less night cold.

When Luis and Freya just now poked in at her door, they launched her party. Momentarily away from them in her kitchen, so crowded it qualified as a kitchenette, they followed her to offer to help, which she nixed. Next, in a clean plate from her kitchen shelf, she glanced in its shine to see if their kisses mussed up her hair. She double-checked in a wide chrome handle, a soup or stew ladle. She was okay.

Sipping a gin and tonic, he, and a Margarita, she, Ian and Candace, now snapped in next to Cait. Cait was stirring her stews. Ian and Candace offered to help stir. What if she must introduce the two pairs, Ian and Candace to Luis and Freya, or Erika, whatever her name was, and their names slipped away?

Fortunately, she did not have to. While stirring, Ian clicked with a black-mustached fellow who stuffed himself into the kitchen. They chatted about the period he and Candace spent in East Africa. They had coincided with plague and famine. So dire were their surroundings that the pair hoped a drought would give way to a flood, as prophesied by soothsayers, shamans, scientists, and priests. Since the Sahara as a prairie died down, fewer centuries had passed than might pass, not necessarily in the distant future. Then the ocean could cover the desert, its sand on the ocean bottom, leaving his wife's Benin on a peninsula between the Atlantic and the Mediterranean. This sea change, he conjectured, would require something tantamount to an ark for survival, two by two.

Actually, Ian and Candace, their very beginning together came to pass in an international hotel. Between conference calls in Washington, D.C., they watched his unrolling of a fifteenth-century Ethiopian Coptic canvas that a poor man sold him. "See how these eyes stare," Ian prompted, "from a once live family."

Cait was drawn to this striking couple and children on the maroon and gray terrazzo, as she was to the now live ones who gazed at the canvas on the floor.

With her eyes, Candace was pinning down the painted couple. Her soft white gauze she wore at the time flounced a bit like a tutu below her small turban in orange, yellow, and greens. Ian asked Candace, "Are you Nigerian?"

"The dress is traditional Ethiopian, but I'm Bini." Her words crisped the air. They clarified her stance.

"Ah, Ms., examine this ancient canvas." He crouched down to examine it.

"Dr.," she corrected, "Dr. Ngambe."

"Oh, sorry."

On the lower steps up to the gallery, Cait saw her eyeing him and penetrating the canvas eyes, until she asked him, "Did you bring it out from Ethiopia to appraise it?"

"Yes, to the first part and, no, about its value. You give me an idea for an appraisal. The crimson's beautiful, don't you agree?" His words bounced from his plumy beard.

* * *

The contents of the three stew pots in Cait's kitchen, one peppery, the other one not so much so, and one to come all simmered on the stove. The red and black mustached men would mix them from time to time.

Peeping in on her other guests throughout her RR long apartment, she savored their gathering that buzzed with everyone sipping ale and wine. She almost danced back into her pale olive-green dining alcove. There she dropped onto an old, spindly wooden chair. Chewed by her older son's basset hound puppy, it once served her great-grandmother while milking cows. Candace sat across from Cait on a matching chair and spoke with a West African cadence.

Cait caught her articulacy in English, French-inflected, when Candace said this to her. "I'm sorry your father just died. Mine cannot last long; he's 96 and lives in Benin City. I'm his youngest."

Ever the interviewer, who avoided self-disclosure, Cait drew out her guest with gesture. "He sent me to a convent school with German nuns who taught me to scrutinize texts and scrub everything dusty, helpful skills for a medical doctor. Most of all, whether rich or not, we'd rely on our resourcefulness.

"From his six wives, my father gained 18 children. He told me to do the best I could, nothing easy." Lifting one of her supple boots, she crossed her legs and jiggled it. After she earned her marketing degree, her first husband, an assistant English and African literature professor at Ann Arbor, fell ill and wished to return to their Benin.

There he became a lecturer, and she managed the first supermarket in the capital, their three children, and his care.

"West African women are known for their marketing," Cait slipped out and said, worrying about monotinting them. Candace nodded. "West Africans," Cait dared on, "party with extraordinary hospitality I know about from a musicologist who's been everywhere and said so." There, better.

"Everyone says so," Candace tuned in. "West Africans love to give everyone a good time with dancing, music, and food, all unimaginable. But if trouble appears, they prefer to disappear."

Soon an unknown virus curtailed her husband's lecturing. Her three older brothers, all doctors, wished to advise her, but her ill husband avoided all doctors, including her brothers, and all treatment.

"Can I assist you with your stews?"

Cait welcomed her offer. She also thought that the pigeons she believed were outside were revving up their chorus, even in the early evening when they were reminding her of reality. Somehow in a reversal of day with night, multi-colored, flickering in beauty, they cooed.

One stew Cait kept simmering on the stove, Napoleon's favorite, with chicken, dark olives, tomatoes, and spices, needed tasting. The other Cait suffered over. Its beef contained coconut milk, curry, okra, and required peanut butter or oil. Guests might not like the spices of one or the other. Neither might blend or even mix enough for anyone's palate.

Candace was sipping the liquid from the ladle Cait

handed her when Ian entered the alcove. To pass the two women in its almost too narrow passage, he scrunched in. Cait breathed in high and thin and climbed on her step stool to reach the peanuts she'd ground days before. She asked this. "Why don't you go into the living room and enjoy yourself? We'll taste and finish the stew."

"In a few minutes." He ducked out.

"Then my first husband," Candace continued. "By the way, very tasty. Let me see the peanuts...."

"My husband then insisted we go back to America. Tentatively I agreed. First, I consulted my father and he, his gods. In his advanced age, he placed replicas of them near him, his bed and stool. More than any of us, he was nearing death and therefore, perhaps, to the gods. My then-living husband, and children, listened to my father, his father-in-law and their grandfather as if to his gods that actually are not idols but aspects of one universal god.

"His six wives each addressed their gods as well. Two are Islamic and bow to Allah. Two are Catholic, one, my mother, prays to God and the Mother. One follows the animist faith of our forebears. The other, like myself, is undecided. My husband was pagan in some respects, though more Catholic. In his varied roles, my father and his several wives supported our plan to go for help, as did my brothers and sisters."

"Are his wives aspects of one universal wife?" Ian asked Candace. At that, Ian, whisking his beard with his thumb, urged his wife to visit the living room.

"You could see to these peanuts, dear." She replied. He strolled on.

Hearing out Candace reminded Cait that she had

accompanied a friend to a Vatican High Mass with cardinals. This friend wished God to reveal her prospects for a happy marriage with her fiancé. "At a highpoint in the mass, the Kyrie, I believe, the unexpected happened. A sailor pinched her bottom. She leaped, singling out his act as an omen."

Candace's words burst out. "No! Did she marry the sailor or her fiancé?"

"Who knows?"

As it turned out, the doctor brothers disapproved of Candace and her then spouse using their savings to fly back to Amerique, where they rented a small house. Her earnings paid for it. As a nurse's aide, she served in the hospital that treated him. After a year, he improved.

Cait perked up. "For you to devote yourself to him, he must have been a good man. As for mine, before I could conceive a third child, mine left for another. Her children played with mine. He specialized obstetrics, and she in pediatrics."

His brief return to pack his clothes and goods little affected the numbed Cait. Oddly, she noted, "He, the sun, blinded me, so I could no longer see."

Candace piped up, "En Afrique, we do not sneak around, as you do here."

"Oh," Cait said, "But they don't anymore. I mean we don't."

Candace pointed out, "My one husband had one wife. He was deathly ill from the virus. If he died, I'd rear my children alone. Yes, he was worth helping.

"People here follow their impulses faster than polygamy can follow. The gods of theology back down. So, folks follow biology."

She added, “Woman may do better under polygamy.”

Cait pried, “Polygamy’s like alimony?” With neither, she dickered over what-ifs.

“Could be,” Candace replied. “When we’d nearly paid off our medical debts, my husband died.”

“I’m sorry.”

“That’s life and grief. I decided to go to nursing school, but a professor counseled me to go to medical school. Then I would learn to treat my husband’s AIDS in others. My aged, though advanced, father sent his support and welcomed my two almost teen children back to his household.”

Instantly, Cait imagined a series of grand thatched straw halls and rooms, much like aged oaks forming a high, outdoor cathedral or summer tent colony. There people cooled whether they strolled in or out. She sang out, “In the forest around here inside the city, a mynah-like bird, a yellow-breasted chat, was calling my name, Cait, Cait.”

“Yes, yes, we call such birds consciences or souls.”

“In my belief, my father was calling me.”

“If you heard our touraco, you’d assume the cuckoo had flown out of the cuckoo clock, because of its squeal.”

“Hello, dear,” she spoke to her husband, Ian.

“I thought my father had flown the grave,” Cait confided. “When I ate dinner with friends on a boat, I sensed him on deck.”

“Yes, mine is here, as if he’d died already.” Candace looked impish.

* * *

Reappearing in the dinette from the kitchen, Ian seemed to ignore the crustiness in his wife's voice, when she said, "We're just talking." The kitchen was still decreasing in space from the enlarged number of individuals who rotated in to take their turn at stirring the stews and, then, out.

Quickly, he caught on to Candace's remarks he'd heard before and ignored her crustiness and voiced his own. "Then she met me. I was a recent American, not yet a member. Gerald MacDonald, a Scots-English psychiatrist, if you like, turned epidemiologist."

After public health experience in Africa, she practiced family medicine again in New York and again in Africa, where she headed an international medical team, as its chief. Ian later joined it and eventually her as her husband.

* * *

When his eyes stared at Cait, she wished she'd stayed secretive about her divorce. She galloped from room to room, checked the sound, whether Bach or Basie, depending on the temperature of the talk. As she next stirred her pots, she wished she possessed a spouse. Her husband used to go back and forth between one end and the other while she tended the food; not that she failed to entertain their guests. Four of the thirteen now present sat on her mission sofa, oversized for three people. Good, they were gesticulating, debating, relating, whatever people do at a party. Ladling the liquid and tasting it, she felt her thoughts ripple along. Stew's almost ready. So, mix the vinegar with herbs and oil for the salad dressing, bubbling tiny rainbows. She recalled Ian, as he presented his case. "One needs," he had said to the pros at his seminar in the audience, "to share one's deepest feeling life with someone else."

The conferees had sat in a bare room on stiff chairs, as Cait stayed on hers, as if the front table constrained her to stay put and listen. She was moved and more. In spite of her job to cover his subject, she'd fled to the toilet stall to sob about the end of marriage, though she was glad to be rid of it. No one else would bother to listen.

She sat on the pot and reflected that its slope down began when her one-time husband lost one of his best friends. He and two other men sat in a circle in the kitchen, and he wet his eyes over their loss. Then he left for his girlfriend. Later at the conference, on the toilet, she was relieved that the toilet paper absorbed her filled eyes, not the shiny kind that prickles when dabbing. She commanded her sadness and fury to cease, for her work habits curved like the ups and downs of sadness and happiness. Her composure reclaimed; she left her stall only to hear Ian speaking in what sounded to be a British-accented African language.

* * *

Here in her apartment, she could gauge the nonchalance of the others. Ian roved back into the kitchen as she stood on one of the spindly chairs to reach a bowl and platters for the stews. "You're looking very decorative." He paused near her calves to comment. Cait held onto whatever fortitude she could muster and was sweating in her Mexican cotton dress as she laughed off this Oxonian invading her privacy over her stove. She shooed him off.

His wife checked back on her husband in the kitchen. He left to circle back to the living room at the end of the long hall. She sauntered out. He returned to say, "Your books are eclectic." Or maybe he said, "excellent." All she could remember on the shelf were ROXANA, NANA, MADAME BOVARY and ANNA KARENINA. She turned the burner under the bun warmer to extra low.

"Candace loves your Tiffany lamp," referring to her one and only treasure—her grandmother's reading lamp with the glass shade.

Cait checked Napoleon's chicken dish. Outside the window, she believed she heard the morning doves cooing in the evening as she stretched up for the goblets, crystal she never used on the top shelf. She wished she'd washed them or hired someone to do so. "Can I help?"

"No." She believed her skirt too filmy. The bell clanged in her ear, a timer informing her to remove the buns. The front door rang. In ran

her two towheads, Barnaby and Joey, with Lulu, a neighboring eight-year-old curly-haired brunette from down the apartment hall. Three grown-ups followed them in the front door. Ian told her, "I invited them. They wanted to meet your guests. I knew you wouldn't mind." When the children insisted on cocoa with their supper, he offered to make it for them.

She was about to place the food on the table for the buffet when he pointed to a vase. "Candace has her heart set on one of these."

Next, she overheard Freya whisper to Candace, "You'd better keep an eye on Ian, don't you think?"

"Oh, I do. Only an eye."

By the time Cait was serving the treacle to those who remained seated with no room to get up and move toward it, Ian approached her and spoke to her neck regarding, "an excellent meal." Distracted and twisted to respond to another compliment, the Englishman stole her back by nabbed a bit of her behind.

Bussed, goosed, and flustered, she sallied forth to her pantry to get her pot of coffee. En route she noted that the children were taking care of themselves in their bedroom. With the coffee in one hand and the apricots in brandy in her other, except for Ian's with prunes, she snuck back in, glad to be back in the living room.

Pairs

Late in a ninety-degree May, Polly was chiding, "I avoid happy people on Memorial Day. You're not too wired to enjoy this scene, are you?" From the green deck toward the scene, the sun was sizzling into the Sound. The light rays flocked through the rigging and sails like veiling. Flags, ropes, and nets crisscrossed the melon red sundown.

Polly bumped her chair as she popped up from the table, clanging the next metal table. Undulating after the waiter for fast service, she rushed. Green stripes and rose blooms accented her bosom and bottom, together like a multicolored windsock. Returning, Polly buzzed, "He's coming."

"Back to what I was saying, we need consoling. But to rope a group together for Memorial Day, you must re-re-re-confirm with each person."

* * *

For camaraderie and relief from work, Elinor lunched with Polly. Dressed in fishnet over red-orange, Polly urged her to drive out to the shore with Robert, known from work.

Both women researchers had retrieved papers from the archives' vault, until Elinor moved on. Polly began breathing life into history.

Welcomed as a patron and sponsor, Robert frequented the archives. Their boss pressed her to nudge him awake at his seat. Aged forty and near the national archival volumes he preferred to the internet, he often snoozed.

* * *

After two hours of driving his Chevy Impala and snoring, she reacted. “Should I sleep at the wheel?" So, they stopped, and he paid for juice and iced tea for alertness.

His sluggishness prompted her back to the wheel. For minutes, they joked awake. Polly was piloting the car as a plane. Punching buttons, she'd ask, "Where're we going?" The plane would tilt toward the ground but swoop to her summer cottage.

En route, Elinor and Robert probed the future. The economy might dive. A onetime securities analyst, now an independent broker, he played on his computer and studied antiques. Suddenly, he asked, "What do you do?"

"Assistant attorney with tenants."

"Good. But watch out. Our technology's shifting. People will someday soon stamp out their wish, their brainchild."

“Stamp?"

"No, there'll be more room for non-matter. Whatever boat, car, or plane you want, if you know what I mean." Abruptly, he slept, until he awoke to reflect on his mother's get-up-and-go. "My great mother and good father cared for me. Since his death 15 years ago, I talked with her every day. A great talker and listener, she was never sick until the end. One day, I rushed too late to see her alive," Robert lamented. "She'd always backed me." His brown hair curled over his forehead, while his brown striped shirt pulled out of his tan pants' waist with his breathing. His mother's collected Venetian glass and Victorian chairs needed authenticating in the archives before selling them.

"Maybe I should have held onto her treasures to hedge against a letdown in the economy. But I sold them to dealers. In their display windows, I saw her glass and chairs, selling for two-thirds more than my earnings. I'm pissed they devalue them. Her chair's worth more than its tag says."

Morose, Elinor still dreamed of her mother on her maroon sofa. On its tufted armrest, her hands and arms lay ridged, veined, and melanin-spotted from gardening. Her mother withered, until the sofa back and seat, like lips, swallowed her. "The loss inside me aches."

"Huh," he gruffed. Snoring, he snorted, woke up to his sound, sat straight. "Know anyone smart who wants a baby?"

Her gloom lifting from her belly, covered by her orange T-shirt and filled with iced tea, her bladder was ready to gush out before another rest stop, was pressing against her seat belt. Complying with laws, Robert had installed it in his pre-seat-belt era car. Elinor was still driving while giddy about Polly as if a-tip in her prop plane. The speedometer informed his tomcat car was speeding. Slowing down, she ordered him, "Wake up!"

* * *

He bolted up. The windmill marked the turnoff to Polly's. Her Dutch door upper half was open. Her note read, "At the shore to swim."

Robert sank into the deck chair he found inside Polly's place and slept.

Rapping at the door, a man, bare from the belly button up, asked, "Party here tonight?"

"Polly's at the beach."

"On the beach tonight?"

Catching her unfriendly voice, Elinor tried, "No, here. Milo's your name?" "No, Milo." "Emil?" "Emile." "French?"

"Mother." His blue eyes glinted within the brown ruff around his chin and head. "Can these critters go in the fridge?" He shelved four live lobsters and three crabs there and left.

Soon, Polly arrived back at her place. The two women set out on foot for the trading post. Its pine interior and baked apple cinnamon muffin aromas welcomed their buying muffins, tomatoes, broccoli, pasta, and cheeses for her hot dish.

Elinor asked, "Who's Emile?"

"A painter friend's matching him with his loft mate, Win. Her style crosses Arthur Dove and Diego Rivera." Such range—Dove's small abstract-blooded Rising Moon and Rivera's giants on the Empire State Building—confused Elinor.

Polly added, "I'm helping Robert search for a mother for his unborn child."

* * *

In her public history youth project, she'd created rabbits multiplying and overtaking Coney Island. Each child from the audience bobbed like a rabbit. In another, a tableau, Verrazano, the explorer, was sighted New York before landing. Her forthcoming program would display current families in colonial New York houses, visited by ghosts of historical figures.

Back from the trading post, at the summerhouse in the woods were the loft artist and spouse in summer white and a couple of neighbors, who soon left for another party. Polly bussed them and hooted, "Robert, how about acting in my show with Elinor as ghosts?"

Robert grumped, "Naw."

Through the glass wall and screen on a track, Win pirouetted into the living room and trilled, "Food! Great! Nobody much cooks these days, except gourmets." Her sleeveless silk over-blouse, blue-like the early night outdoors, divided her in two in the room's dim light. Her yellow skirt flared around her with its dots inked in like holes into nighttime. As if to bow, she threw her long skirt up above her knees, sitting across from Robert.

Polly introduced him as a securities analyst to this Oklahoma artist. Polly presented Elinor as a lawyer. Polly was pleasing Elinor, though mistaken.

With three hooks and eyes on a rubberized belt cinching her waist, Win settled down to reveal her calves. "I can't stand my boss with the power to punch us to push sales."

"Get another job," Robert recommended. From hours of sleep, his dark eyes pinched less than earlier, and hair shone in the lamplight. Win and Robert bickered over her leaving her job.

Polly chirped. "Win, everyone who's come to this land feels put upon or persecuted." Everyone listened.

After greeting Polly, Emile leaned to test a pan of water to boil for pasta, lobsters, and crabs, and poured rosé from Robert. "French," asked Polly.

"French immigrant mother and Connecticut founder. My mother ran my father's life. She's dying and he's a flounder caring for her. Blinking, Emile exited and flattened himself on his car hood and windshield in the heat.

Robert was winning his battle against slumber and rediscovering his belly. "Elinor, let's go buy food and more wine." Polly, he claimed, was too disinterested in food to trust a meal to get itself onto her long oak table. Elinor rattled some pans to signal a meal in the making.

Others sprawled in the heat, and Emile bounded off his car to turn off the pots of water steaming. From the freezer, he grabbed lobsters, their pincers stuck, also pulling out frozen ice cube trays.

"They'll defrost," Elinor said, fanning herself. In this heat, Polly must be replaying the Battle of Long Island with firepower. She pleaded for a fan, scouted in her closets, found one, plugged it in and angled it at peoples, slouching and buzzing.

Win was circulating. "Now I loathe my job; ten years ago I loved my career. I was a fashion plate and coordinator." Home for Win was alongside a famed fashion photographer, lasted 16 years and ended two months ago.

Hearing over the fan clicking every so often, Elinor asked, "He ran off with a 16-year-old?" But Polly overheard and asked, "You met him at 16?"

"Now, he's with one who looks 16. I need a friend. Sex bores me." Emile turned. Her black cap of hair shone in the candlelight, as she swooshed her bright yellow skirt with the midnight polka dots from side to side. Sitting on Polly's couch armrest, he inquired, "If you met him at sweet 16, how old are you?"

Displaying one of her calves, she ignored him. "Daddy passed before my birth. Somebody has to pay the bills, not my family. My mom's visiting from Oklahoma, pays her way. With a gorgeous girl, my gorgeous, tall, blond brother, won't pay. He's opening a hair salon out here."

Elinor observed Win's brother must have blunt cut and hennaed her hair dark red. Win stepped into the toilet to replace her sweaty red Tee with navy and onlookers could see she'd fastened only one of seven hooks and eyes. Was she conjuring that life was imaginary?

For the lobster feast, Emile neared her to stack dishes on the table. He replied to her query about his work. "I'm a restorer, who's refurbishing *The Sun Also Rises*." Know it? Everybody around here does. The owner's gay and inscribed a blow-up of Hemingway on the wall, 'Dear Kai, if only we'd known each other.'"

"Some friends, forsaken by others, could say the same. They wound up in Sing-Sing or on the street. Hemingway unwound in bullpens and fishing boats. He used to flex his calves, like this." Emile also swayed from one calf to the other and sipped some Mattes from a half globe-shaped goblet. Also, he yanked up his pelvic muscles to shake them loose, like a dog stretch before shimmying.

"I like his Pilar," commented Elinor.

"I've discovered Sappho," Emile added. "What's left, as it's 'un-gathered.' Perfect."

He dropped the crabs and lobsters headfirst into the pot of boiling water. They turned red-orange, as Win was beguiling Robert or Emile. "My work combines Dove and Rivera influences."

"How'll we crack the lobster?" Elinor asked Polly. "A nutcracker?"

"I haven't eaten lobster in years. Use the hammer."

Win asked Robert, "Do you have a private practice?"

"I once thought about that. I'm not that kind of analyst."

"Are you a couple?"

"On the couch? Who?"

"Polly?"

"Nah."

"The other?"

"No, our mothers just died."

"Sorry. I'm going to see mine in the next town."

"It's awfully late."

By 10:30 pm, they were nibbling appetizers, until the serving of the lobsters when Win ducked out to light up her cigarette red in the dark. Polly whisked her rigatoni into the pot, vacated by the lobsters, with broccoli, draining them for a platter. She plopped sauce from a bottle and melted cheese on the pasta. Elinor banged the lobster shell to fork out morsels to dip in the melted butter.

"God, it's great to eat again." Win admired.

"I want to bless our food," Polly declared. "May it nurture us."

Extending his fork for lobster and crab, Emile asked

Elinor, "Aren't we atheists or agnostics here?"

"Skeptics?"

"Or ghosts, if we don't eat!" Polly commanded. "Food awaits us."

"I need a friend," Win mouthed between lobster and broccoli. To herself, Elinor was betting Win would bear Robert's baby.

Outside, not even lightning bugs dotted the hot night. No moon. Under the lamp, Robert was swatting insects as Emile leaped through the door to turn on jazz on his car radio and his headlights, floodlighting the living room through the sliding walls.

"Keep the bugs and lights out," Polly called out, "when you return." He snapped off the headlights and came in.

Win left from the veranda to go out to smoke. He followed her out again and said, "We've kissed."

"That was a friendly goodnight."

"We could stay together."

"But we don't know each other."

"Who cares." He was hidden. Inhaling her lit, orange-tipped cigarette revealed her in the dark.

Breathing through his mouth and dozing, Robert gulped a bug. "Ach!"

Polly asked Win, "Whatever happened to your loft mate and his wife?"

Win shrugged and noted, "If I'd insisted on sharing my feelings, as she does, my life with the great one would have ended after 16 weeks. My loft mate's wife slows them down. I prefer a man who rarely shares feelings and needs no shoring up." She bounced her stacked sandal and wiggled her painted dark toe to the jazz.

Clapping, Polly gushed. "If we don't share, how do we pick up that we're all units of each other. In crises, we pull farther apart."

"When the couple in white," Emile proffered, "blew in, I was on my car. They were arguing. They left together and never returned."

"Un-gathered," commented Elinor.

"When people drop their feelings," Polly lilted, "others grab and hold them. When the mother of the man who contains mine was dying, I spent days and nights with his sadness. After she died, he looked at me across the room and said, 'I'm coming into some money, so I'll look for a younger woman.'"

"So, I collect others, rabbits and ghosts." Polly saluted anyone who would listen. "I'm my own self." Toward Elinor, she winced and waved a little wave.

Moments later, Emile and Win were stirring to leave in separate cars. Win chided Emile for driving on too much wine. She'd drive and drop him at home, before going to her mother.

Worn out, Elinor strolled past the bedroom, were Robert was snoring. Running after her, Polly whispered, "El, all this gives rise to what we don't yet know. Robert indicates you'd be right as the mother of his baby."

On Sunday morning, Robert said, "I feel great. Let's leave soon. I've got a party this afternoon. I'll drive." They bussed Polly good-bye.

Portfolio

During the deluge early in the spring, Sybil stayed home from the children's theatre. To distract herself from boredom while exercising, she pulled on the tele-computer knob and lay flat on the floor. Surprisingly, the daily program introduced Victoria Jason at a civic forum on drainage. Fanning upright from the floor, Sybil watched a phantom from her past.

Years earlier, in junior high, students had nick-named Sybil, "Syb" or "Sybelly" and the telecommentator Victoria, "V.J." Grown-ups called her "Vichy." A Greek exchange student, Sybil's friend, identified Victoria, as "the classical American woman."

When everyone else was lumpy, some might have appraised her as the ideal. But they hardly bothered to pare themselves down. Besides, Victoria straightened up to six feet tall to see everyone. Anyone as tall and slight-framed without flab as Victoria could only look boned.

Thirteen-year-old Sybil was asked to care for Vichy's children. V.J. lived on the square court, a street crinkled-paved around the park to discourage cars. Her home was fenced back-to-back with Sybil's family home and her parents' garden. She helped weed beans, cucumbers, onions, tomatoes, carrots, rhubarb, and cabbages, all fortified by compost.

But Victoria, neighbors claimed, was too exotic to plant even carrot seeds in the ground or a petunia in a terra cotta pot. She would water her yard but never weed. In fact, she implanted bio-tex, developed in a lab for velvety lawns. Some few disapproved. Velvet pollen could blow everywhere.

Most people in town sprang from the soil. But Vicky, the homegrown foreigner, had gone to New York, returned to marry and give birth to her babies, and aimed to go back there as her career flowered.

* * *

Now Sybil trespassed through a neighbor's yard to the V.J. door. Unlocking it, she let it fall against Sybil and said, "Careful. The loose screen wire might snag my crepe."

Her periwinkle dress matched her eyes. She peroxided her hair into platinum to set off her phosphate blue eyes and nitrate red, lush mouth. Her eyes lavish with a tin gray streak over red-brown shadow so enlarged, they half-masked her face.

To try to befriend her, Sybil gushed, "beautiful shoes."

"They're Florentine," V.J. replied. "Each toe was measured, and these shoes were crafted to fit."

* * *

Victoria Jason's TV show was beamed during Sybil's youth to their part of the Mid-Heart area of the country. On it, Victoria modulated her voice and modeled new treasures of bravura gowns.

At thirteen, understanding her minimal standing,

Sybelly was agog. Only a babysitter, she pretended to be an au pair from another country. “Au pair,” she repeated to herself, “Au pair.”

Her best friend was going off with her father and his third bride’s children to a North Atlantic island honeymoon. Having invited the Greek student to go, not Sybil, her best friend was no longer her best friend.

* * *

Still, the V.J. world of TV, joining the computer, fascinated Sybil, however miffed at being left behind by her onetime friend. As for duties, V.J. said. "Your friend must have told you about our four- and six-year-olds to care for."

Not really. Anyway, on this day, V.J.'s husband would pick up the oldest from camp. Today, Sybil would iron out wrinkles.

The "brats," V.J. reminded her, "are in the pan for boiling for the children. Take one for yourself for lunch."

Victoria departed for her show. Sybil began her other assignment of ironing out wrinkles in their sheets and undies, until her arm ached. In her intermission, in the hall, she peeked at tiers of glossies. Sybil scrutinized close-ups of the onetime Tower model, the many Victorias. In one, the dark dress was molded on V. V. could not have unzipped it. She'd have had to unravel it. If V. held her breath, her rib cage subbed for a bosom.

Victoria's photos on one wall faced her husband's. In his, he punted, kicked, and he received a loving cup.

* * *

Suddenly, up from nap time, banging overhead their child bumped down the stairs on his bottom. A curly top, he begged, "Play with me?" With the ironing finished, she'd play.

Dropped off from camp, his older brother climbed the stairs and flushed the toilet.

In those days, babysitters and babies, no technicians swabbed their mouths of saliva to measure cortisol, since it might detect whether an adult benefits the child. This enzyme tie measure between the newborn and baby nurse, other comforter, especially the father or mother, could assure, it was said on ads, enough nurture and trust for the infant. If love gapped between nurturers and child, the nurse or sitter filled in.

Sybil was a stand-in, she knew. Freddie and Georgie had just lost their giggly sitter and challenged Sybil.

* * *

Hours later, Vichy, back from her show, screamed. "See the mush on my dining table!" From the toilet overhead, tissue plopped there. Liquid was splotching the dark mahogany.

Sybil herself blanched and was fired.

Later, her uncle intoned that the poor finish on the table could little resist discoloring. Watermarks marred the finish. Her parents, he said, should take V.J., Vichy, to Small Claims Court for Sybil's wages.

* * *

At the moment, with a TV video of this episode

implanted in her head, Sybil exercised before the vision. Ticking off time, Victoria, body less a twig and more a branch, tarried in Chicago with her throaty comments.

Her husband had died, and her children had grown. On Chicago TV, Vichy ticked off extra time learning Russian, along with Spanish. Next, assigned to Moscow to chronicle the return of the Romanovs, within her chinchilla and dyed matching mink high hat, she advanced in expertise back to New York, where Sybil also lived.

* * *

Meanwhile, Sybil was transferring the Children's Mugwump Theater to TV computing. Children were improvising with contents they could flush onto a mahogany table in a sketch for child mutiny.

Balloons

He had one green eye and one dark brown, both focused and intense beneath his yellow hair. His best friend, Marty, told him he was giving a party for all his best friends. Bobbie was maddening but never got mad much at Marty, nor they at each other, though some others battled with each of them or both. "Too much lip," his grandmother claimed about both of them.

Some said, mostly big people, that it was rumored that Bobbie was impossible. Therefore, his presence at the party would lead them to forbid their kids going to her party. Because of his bashing other boys with words or fists, they had to consider him an adult almost. Not only that, in effect Marty said someone told him that someone else pissy-whispered that Bobbie's green eye came from the whites in his Euro family and the darker brown-black one from his Carob mother.

Marty's mother decided the only thing to do was to ask her best friend what to do about her party and which kids to invite, so he would giggle and jump for joy at his own party for Halloween and birthday at age seven. He would call Bobbie up and invite his big sister, Marie, who would guard him. Linda, Marty's mother, wiped out from her job as a monitor on research projects and underpaid, wished for a just-so Halloween-birthday.

The big and small one gabbed over details, such as, orange vs. chocolate cookies. A chocolate cake or mocha and vanilla swirl, lit with eight candles, would contain a wrapped surprise dropped into the batter. Once baked and served at the party, whoever almost ate the prize would win another prize, maybe a bag of other treats or tiny comics. His eyes pinched, when he thought of a piñata with more surprises to fall on his friends.

* * *

Yes, they would show a very scary movie. He named some. These names blurred in his mother's head, more so in the heat of an Indian Summer. Still, they needed to ask everyone to wear costumes. "Scary," Marty reminded her.

"No, we'll take boxes," he referred to those of his buddies and a few girls. "The make-pretend clothes from Grandma's attic'll give every kid a chance to pick stuff to put on." His mother countered that he must consult Grandma about her belongings. "She will let me," he insisted.

"What will yours be?" Linda asked her son. From their front closet, he picked a dark gray pointy hat, at the front indented for thumb and forefinger, once belonging to his dead grandfather. Along with a cane, he donned it and grimaced while deciding to be a spy or a detective. He'd wear a half-mask or a kerchief over his mouth, and he pointed his finger.

They agreed, then, on his guests coming in their costumes and he in his. If anyone forgot, they would somehow provide a mishmash of old clothes to concoct a costume.

Two days ago, his mother had cut from her own

pattern black and white satin for a Harlequin outfit with a neck ruffle, which he could wear. "Nah, too fancy. Give it a girl." He wanted to be a private eye. So, Linda put on a long top, ruffled at the neck, to see if it suited her.

If no hobgoblins came, he went on that he would be disappointed. Because they might, they did not, he insisted, need to clean up his and his mother's little house. "The house'll be messy when they leave, so why fix it up?" Still his mother pressed him to help.

When he spilled a pail of water and pine oil on the floor, she screamed at him. He tried mopping it up. She threatened to send him to his father's house for two weekends in a row, instead of their every other one. His parents had divorced when he was three-and-a-half years old.

"Who's caring for me tonight?" he blurted. His blue eyes watered beneath his curly light brown hair, like his father's. Already he reached her elbow. She knew from child studies that boys about finish crying by fifth grade. Marty, not yet.

"You and Bobbie are hobgoblins." She teased him, as she tried to hug him. They blew up orange pumpkins with a gas pump. On most they inked on devilish faces for a ceiling covered with heads. Others they saved for the guests to do.

"They can pop," he declared, "when we show the scary movie to make everyone jump."

* * *

Blinking, she flipped through video lists: "The Mummy, was a Vampire,"

"Ghoul in Hiding," "Warlock in the Third Ring." Scratching his hair, Marty went along with opposing any video about the devil. They bickered about which video.

He had heard about "The Burning Bed." She nixed it. Next, he begged for "Halloween." That might work. Marty was also happy his dad planned to bake a devil's food cake with the penny in tinfoil to surprise someone. He told his father, also blue-eyed, that his whole class was coming to his Halloween-birthday party, now that he, Marty, was the best-liked in his class.

* * *

Everything almost in place, the bell rang. Gypsy arrived first. She was wearing gold hoop earrings and gold lame blouse over black. When Artist arrived in her red beret and black turtleneck over black tights, Marty worried that only girls were flooding his party. Worse yet, no one would be scary.

Too busy to bother, his mother was sweeping up nail clippings and hair locks from her haircuts and swabbing the bathroom in their small frame two-bedroom house. When his father carried in the chocolate cake on a tray, Marty was more excited by the big man's costume. He praised his father as a gangster. He shouldered a navy raincoat that opened to two tacked-on shoe bags with many interior pockets for bottles of booze. His dad's black fedora tipped onto his eyes above his ashy beard and mustache. His height, though, ran into one of the crepe paper streamers and pulled it down.

His mother had earlier pulled out a nail, tacky in her view, from the wall, where a streamer or Christmas pine wreath usually got tied up. Everything belonged where it lay, except the streamer, so to re-tape the fallen one, she swept out of the toilet. Her hair was bright like brass platinum. Black satin, studded with brilliants, masked her face, except her mouth, where blood painted her lips, and glued on inch-long fingernails. Her harlequin costume fit her, like the hugs she gave Marty. He squealed, “You look weird!”

New bell rings later, he whooped over Cowboy from next door and Bobbie with his 14-year-old sister. In powdered hair, she dressed in nets and webbing, like a Miss Havisham, and Bobbie, not quite Pip, like a Chimney Sweep with broom. Next Witch and Warlock strolled in black clothes, pointy hats, and fingernails all silvery. Marty was overjoyed with the scary people.

More arrived. They and the ones there dashed to the table for chips, popcorn, soda, and nuts. Bobbie grabbed them with both hands. His sister pulled his arm back, and he revolted by throwing popcorn. Someone called him, "Caribee." Everyone scattered to pick up the corn kernels, exploded to eat, and the hard ones, unexploded, to pelt at each other.

* * *

Linda flipped on another light and the CD player for loud music. She vied with the hoopla to win them to using magic markers to create more balloon heads. At the same time, girls jiggled in dance. An unknown ghost was making a face on the wall. “No, no,” yelled Linda.

Parents wound their ways in the front door. More children bee-lined for the dining room, and parents settled into the living room. Three paraded in store-bought costumes for Skeletons and a Pirate. The Witch and Warlock paraded with their fellow partygoers and bounced around the room, until Marty screamed, "Video."

Bag Lady plopped in front of it. She complained about the warped floor that tipped Bobbie the Chimney Sweep toward her. "Stop that!" she shouted. "Shut up." The others rebuked her.

Calm overcame them, as they hunched in an irregular circle to watch the film. Gypsy's gold lame reflected light from the living room.

Whether in the dining room on its floor or in the living room, everyone cheered when paper plates with chocolate ice cream arrived and they sang "Happy Birthday." Celebrating it, they ignored Halloween. Marty opened his gifts of cars, trucks, planes, two books, a video game, a huge toy mutt, and jeans.

While the children returned to the video, there sat two former nuns, two former husbands as fathers, three teachers of which two black and one white and several miscellanea. Linda wished to ask what they did or where in their heart, where they belonged. Instead she doffed her femme fatale platinum wig.

Someone was declaiming that the time had not yet come for female boxers or football players. Another said female firefighters could not carry out fire victims.

Still another scoffed. Chimney sweep announced that no boxers came to his party.

The little Old Maid was walking through the living room to the bathroom, as another girl, one of the Skeletons, came out and angled off to touch Linda's niece's dollhouse-to-be, stored with Linda, until Christmas. Restlessness had set in, Linda noticed. As she snapped off the creepy movie, Marty objected. "Everyone likes it." His father had just gone. He resisted her soothing him into saying goodnight to his friends and guests.

The girls in the store-bought clothes helped clean up. The Pumpkin, who'd arrived late, sat waiting to be picked up.

Minutes later, Marty taunted his mother. "You messed up the party. No more Halloween parties." He slumped on the couch, his eyes bloodshot, his skin sallow.

Linda scraped her brain for factors on whether she'd destroyed his party, as he stomped out of the room she'd decorated. After all, everyone invited had turned up, and everyone ate goodies, more than crumbs. "No, no," she reacted to Marty.

"No one will," he declared, "speak to me anymore. Only the girls in the store-bought clothes, and they don't count. And Bobbie with one blue eye and one black eye. Maybe he'll still be my friend."

To pop the un-popped ones, Marty was pitching unexploded popcorn kernels at the orange balloon heads with faces on the ceiling. One by one they were exploding and falling. Some orange ones inked with their features and black balloons with white lines for their features were oozing out their helium, drifting, falling and rolling on the floor.

In the front room, red ones with smiley faces with, "Celebrate," drifted. Back and forth on the ceiling of the two rooms, heads were also bobbing, as the front-door opened and closed, sucking air. "Tomorrow's All Saints Day, you said so," he reminded his mother. "Maybe tomorrow I'll be a floating saint."

Adjustment

3:00 a.m. The phone rang. It did, didn't it? After all, detectives called for lineups after midnight to check whether the attacker from six months earlier stood there. But the end of the line issued silence. The caller hung up.

Dread was overwhelming. Wetness sounded sticky from passing car wheels, as sleep no longer possessed one and the streetlight illuminated the yellow, blue, and green stained-glass window in front of her. She was stiff, though just able to pull herself by grabbing a nearby doorknob to stand to go step by step to reach the window to look out.

Outside, rainwater met a subterranean welling up from the fault line stream near the stone wall. Water overflowed around the knoll crossed by the exit road painted midline.

Sleepless and stuffed up, she leaned over the new metal window frame, paired with another that braced the inserted red and blue stained glass.

Breathing cold air, she studied the knoll in the street that bubbled like an eye shut just so high so as to create a white slit. Arm in arm with her partner in paradise, a pregnant woman, her belly shaped like the eye, bobbled over the knoll street line, and her black coat opened over her white top and pants for partying to create a line vertical to the street. He, dark-coated, was aligned to her side, arm drawn around her and head bent toward hers.

They walked out of sight.

Marike shivered. "A long time since I've cared."

Twenty yards beyond their cross-point, a serrated knife could have sliced off the steep rocky slope. Hobbling back from the windows, she ducked under the bed covers.

Awake still at 4:30 a.m. Up again, she shuffled to the living room. The digital clock, answering machine, VCR, and CD player numbers blinded in red neon.

Slumping on her couch, mossy pillows fell around her and tried to dull her thoughts.

For relief, they traveled back to Dr. N. who re-aroused them against stormy days and stormy nights. After ruining two cheap red umbrellas, she'd carried a third one with a wooden bird head handle to Dr. N's office. There was stiffening into her knees, up her sides, across her lower back, and down the thighs through the knees. The left was worse than the right in an acute phase and inflexible. This stiffness mimicked her mother's paralysis, unless it eased, until it jabbed again with pain. All the pain she'd ever felt, from falling off a bronco and rafting in rocking water and car accidents flushed forward insider at this instant. She named this pain H paresis.

By late morning, she struggled downstairs to the lobby mailbox under the stairs. Rattled, her key jammed in her box.

Jumping when asked the time, she was relieved to see her neighbor. His spectacles enlarged his face. His frame narrowed and shortened, more than hers, into trust. "Could you, please, unlock my box on the bottom row. If I bend, I can't stand back up."

Smiling in spite of his own back agony, he turned her key for her mail. "See Dr. N. I see him. The best, good fellow, my wife says, is good looking and injects something in the spine to ease the pain."

* * *

The detective, Patricio Rodriguez, *si*, had warned Marike, "Stay away from dead-end and odd streets, lobby niches and inside corners like hers with the postal boxes and stairwells. His white *linea* suit served his gallantry; he was still more dashing with his karate gold-edged black belt, worn for teaching and dancing. The belt matched the flare of his mustache. One night, brought home from a police line-up, he directed, 'No hideaways. See, otherwise, flashbacks will overtake you.'"

She'd tried listening. "You're my last call. I'm going dancing now. You'll dance again and come back late!" Swashbuckler in meringue and salsa, he'd ask her, to dance, dance only, only dance.

Back in her apartment, the interior off-light from the sun was sepulchral. Entombed, Marike should get out to Dr. N. and called for an appointment. Not there until Monday, three days away. In that period, her H might improve.

That day Marike dressed in blues, pull-on jeans with a rubber waist she need not zip up or snap and a Prussian blue pullover. She half-crawled five blocks to his office, and once there she declared victory.

White blonde-veiled to her waist, the secretary chirped to patients and phone callers and handed a card to Marike for her data and symptoms, which hurt with every pencil stroke.

The doctor, like all therapists consulted, would be uninterested in her awareness of body stiffness from her mother's paralysis. Still she wrote down her symptoms for Dr. N.

His vision of a secretary directed her to sit next to his office, pine paneled.

In a frame sat or stood five young adults and three tiny children, all photo-beauties. His, she assumed, when he arrived. She tried to compose herself.

She'd expected a thickset round-headed brown-haired man, balding, like her last muscle doctor, seen after the car accident from the flood. But Dr. N. differed. Without helmet or hardhat, his hair reflected lines of silver, and the sight of him stunned her. Other than what she had written on the card, she told her neighbor's wife's Apollo doctor nothing about the origin her semi-paralysis.

Happiness ran with goodness. In his examining room, he suggested removal of her upper garment and tying on the red plastic top. His nurse had already, but she ignored the white-dressed woman. His manner was antiseptic.

Time would tell. He left, and she waited.

In treatment in the next cubicle, the deep-voiced woman ran a booking agency. She and the handsome doctor, Irish-looking, chitchatted about cantors from the 1950s she knew little about from television, including Jackie Gleason, Eddie Fischer, Richard Tucker, and before TV, J.S. Bach, Protestant cantor. Listening, Marike, feeling not so much Irish, started to laugh in pain and wished to tap-dance.

But she stared at the wall with Dr. N's medical certificates and licenses.

This doctor, unlike her last, offered more than a stretcher, a black leather device, slanted from floor to ceiling or parallel with it, daunting her now that she was on it. Her feet paralleled the ceiling, or could tip, feet up. Harm possible wracked her mind. Its cushion, soft, leathery, signified less than horror. Strapped on the rack, she could be mounted face down.

"Only a moment, I'll be back," his voice rumbled. When he returned, he injected a substance seemingly into her neck to end her overall stiffness, as her stomach dropped to the floor but came back up.

His treatment was finished, just like that, her ultra crick in her neck was gone. She chatted mindlessly and concluded. "I didn't know Jackie Gleason was a cantor."

"Oh yes." The choir leader doctor, august, silvery, and handsome, his warmth contrasted with his erect, correct posture—no H with him—"You'll feel better soon. You will soon laugh. Come back for more treatments." He was watching her—his patient.

Outside, raindrops informed her she'd left her white umbrella behind, but she plodded on home.

For three days, she still avoided going back to her work in human resources with other peoples' troubles and snuck out for food. Getting back home was run for cover.

Later one afternoon, the secretary in his office notified Marike's answering machine that her umbrella was taking up room in the chiropractic lobby. Also, the pen she'd used to write a check for the doctor was needed. So, she called back and asked when to pick up one and drop the other off. The beauty at Dr. N's desk answered, "Dr. N. put the umbrella in the car rear to prevent stealing and will call you about dropping it off."

The next morning, her back improved, she rattled and strolled with cans for recycling and reached the newsstand where she bought newspapers, *Le MONDE* and *CORRIERE della SERA*, to exit from dullness. If she read their Romance languages and studied the photos, goings-on in Paris and Milan would distract her from fear. Far-flung events disturbed her more, her problems troubled less. Riots cheered her. Theft reassured her that the world was gristle, and with suicide or murder, war was more.

The Lebanese news vendor at his window was friendly. A halo must have collapsed on his head, for his hair grew out around his bald spot, like tonsure.

From his jawbone to his mustache, he replied. "*Comment ça va*?"

"*Bien*." She added, "*Comme ci, comme ça, merci*," so thanks, and paid for the papers.

Turning away, she was face to face to Dr. N.'s stare several feet away from his office doorway. Silvery and perfectly toned, he seemed to bow to her, as he said, "You're walking?"

Forgetting to ask about the umbrella, he lay in her mind. Seven weeks of feeling better led her to his office to inquire about her back. The visionary beauty at the front desk, long hair veiling, Serena, the receptionist, told her, "Dr. N.'s out. He gave up on you."

"Here's the umbrella. Doesn't rain fall on you?"

Hearing a male voice, Marike asked to use the toilet

farther into the back rooms; she lingered there before returning to the waiting room to kill time until the male voice materialized. She wondered about what this beauty was to the doctor? His receptionist did rattle on though about her children who presumably knew their father.

Unsure, Marike sat, bending her head around in yoga. If only someone would dynamite her head pressure. Loosen it into pieces.

Back at home again, she studied her mother's crewel wall hanging above her. Two to the trunks writhed into one. Browns, gold, and reds lifted into muted hues of greens, rose, and yellows, as squirrels and birds romped and flew.

Within the turds beneath the trunk, she fell back into memory.

She had hurried along the main avenue as shopkeepers slammed down metal gates over their storefronts. By the greengrocer, plantains hung, apples piled, and sugar cane leaned like bamboo stalks.

Suddenly, car brakes jammed, horns honked, and Marike jumped at the racket that jarred her back to her late evening nightmare. Along the corridor, lights dimmed with smoky nightfall and the street tunneled into a dark hollow.

Heels snapping behind her picked up speed and halted giddiness in bar hopping and joy, finding one last all-night restaurant. On weekends, partygoers crowded this place. On this weeknight, no one danced, no dusky men and women rippled in low cut necklines and skirts or svelte fit ones who by their presence protected her.

In the dead quiet, woman's shoes clapped ahead of her. Marike rushed the formidable street length toward home, while someone galloped behind her. To see, her neck would not turn. Darkness thickened, intensified and she strode on, hoping to reach her goal before it receded. Steps continued as she raced through a mirror and her heart pumped in her toes.

Breathless, she slowed when the steps slowed. She breathed, while the steps did stop momentarily.

Approaching the eye incline, she gripped her big jagged key, resistant to lock-picking, as she struggled to find the smaller key for her building's front door from among too many keys, unnerved her enough to pick the right one.

With someone behind her, she stood aside to give the go-ahead to enter, but he hung back. She slammed the door, or tried to. But the door's valve resisted her closing against him, his foot between the door and its frame and thwarted her closing and locking it. Two heads higher than hers, he forced the door open. She groaned.

He rushed on up the stairs, and to her relief, the elevator arrived and she instantly pressed three. The elevator took off up, though it stopped on the second floor, where the giant forced his way in.

She began to unbuckle her watch, but he was dull in reacting to it. When she handed it to him, he dropped it.

The camera strapped and slung over her shoulder. To protect herself, she handed it to him, but he shook his head.

She pressed the buttons to stop the elevator at each floor. He reached for the stop button. Then she pulled out the large safety pin she carried for trouble.

Nervously, she tried to jab him. But the down of his white jacket was too thick for her pressure to reach him.

Her scream made no sound. He shoved her arm away.

* * *

Next, she reached for the alarm. It started to sound. He pulled out a dagger. Briefly it blinded her. "I have knife. Be careful. You people, this is for you. Lower your pants and turn your back to me."

She stretched for the elevator's warning bell. But he lunged for her arm.

She froze. She let them drop. She bent down. He did not plunge the dagger into her. He did. She bled.

He ordered her to get dressed. She flipped off the stop button and pressed three for her floor. There she stepped out and held the door, where she'd threatened. "I'll get you. Wait and see."

The door had closed against him, and inside her apartment she'd sobbed.

Thank God, her daughters were with their father. The only woman she knew to call was a friend of a friend, Bettina, who told her to call the cops who'd take her to the emergency.

Much later, she realized in Dr. N's waiting room that she'd been hooked up to the plumbing of her time.

Her medium-sized Swiss Army knife in hand at home, she studied its deep red and its small, bright gold cross and began to carry it with her at all times. Shehad pulled out its corkscrew, its scissors and its small blade and finally, its large blade. She would scar the too handsome face of the attacker and his member.

When the phone rang, Marike shook herself awake,

as the mother secretary said to her, "Dr. N. says come to his office this Saturday."

Bewildered and ecstatic in an overlay and underlay, one cannot know what's going on with the other. Her new thoughts focused on Dr. N as her back's H stiffening and headache were dissolving.

* * *

Having exercised her anxiety away, she bolted for his office before she changed her mind about going there. With the ring of his door, he answered. She stammered, "Where's your secretary?"

He chuckled. "I'm alone." He held the door for her. Her knife was in her raincoat pocket. It was.

"Sit down," he said and got lost behind the scenes of curtained niches.

Another ring at the door, someone else's, Marike answered, relieved to see another being.

"You go next," she said to the young man, "I'm early."

"No, you."

Dr. N. returned, and she watched him over the edge of her magazine, as he beckoned to her. "I can wait," she said. "He can go first; I have time to kill."

The bell rang again. She answered it and was surprised to see an ex-priest from her office. Pretending enthusiasm about his back problem and the value of the injection treatment, she nodded.

Dr. N. came out and offered no choice but to follow and make small talk about his family on the wall. He asked, "Are you laughing again?"

"No, tap-dancing."

The Bench

Porter was strolling on the sidewalk toward where the other two were basking in the warm day. On their usual choice bench, Harry Amos and "Blue," otherwise known as Bill Curtis, crossed their legs to the left, swinging them. Matthew, his baptismal name, closed in on them. He preferred to be called "Porter." Guessing he might bump, by accident, into them on the bench while passing, they yanked in their legs. Instead, Porter sat next to them. His foot angled the other way from them to the right. If Blue put his bum leg that way, it cramped. At times, to relieve pressure on his thigh, for flexibility, he first pulled up his tan cord pants or chinos, and switched whichever leg crossed which thigh to the other.

The ups and downs of their legs reminded Blue of his daughter's moods, and lately Porter's. Because of his blue shirts, others took to calling him "Blue." If the wrong item crossed his daughter's mind, it jabbed her, and he noticed her down mood and belly out. Her hair's the wrong color or length, or her face pimpled. Her weight's too stacked, her outfit's not right unless the ultra latest, avant-garde. He, the old pop, knew his cotton plaid shirts belonged to the dead-beat past, as did he and Harry.

He and Harry aired worries about their kids. Porter said he had no kids. The two older guys wondered to each other why a handsome youth, well built beneath his T-shirt and long beard, fathered no kids these days. He seemed, they decided, a little down.

As for his own youngest, Blue would ask Harry and even Porter, if around, "Why couldn't she be ordinary? Like her mother and sisters, could she get her degree, a good job and a home? She's smart ... but seems cursed."

"Good looking too," Harry piped up. Neighbors on the same block, he and his Sally reared their two sons, while Blue with his now deceased wife did so with their three daughters. The first two were launched. Not so with their last one.

Originally, Blue and Harry had waved to each other as neighbors. Much later in their retirement, aged early eighties, they gabbed about their kids, books the two of them read, and the screwy world they all lived in, while sitting on their bench. Blue interpreted to Harry, "These days, young ones worry more than us old folks. Before we've even finished ours, they're feeling their ends near."

"Not yet," Harry countered Blue. "Not me, so soon either."

If only the two of them could catch on to the young. Blue ruminated. What bothered the Lenas of the world, his Lena? Their heads bald or cropped, like Blue's, or hair blanched, dyed black, chartreuse and maroon, or white and blue, or left as was, gave him few clues.

Harry viewed these new types, "through their raves, clubs and whatnot, piercing and cutting, are mutants, like the obese ones and other oddities, 'autists,'" he named others. He and Harry tried to figure these phenomena out.

"Next thing we know," Harry chimed in, "they'll stretch their necks with rings. Not Lena though," he reassured his buddy.

Blue thought to himself. If he could just pin down her trouble, he'd lick it. Or she would. "Before dying," he added, "my Margie called our change-of-life, youngest daughter, Lena, named for her grandmother, "a heart-sick rebel, who blots up sadness around her."

* * *

One day, a few days later, Blue told Harry and Matt Porter that he had knocked on Lena's door. He'd pleaded to her, "How can I help you feel better?"

Withdrawn and slumped on her bed, she faced the wall, mumbling, "Nothing, Dad." Blue strained over her more than he ever had over his sick wife. What if the time came when he could no longer stand on his bum leg, and Lena could still not take care of herself?

Going back in his thoughts, he remembered that at eight, Lena had talked about how she was going to die. By twelve, with puberty and acne, she was suicidal. At odd times though, she perked up and giggled. She startled Margie and Blue again at 16. One on each side of her, they coaxed and coerced her into visiting a psychiatrist. By the time, her mother died, she was 18. He could do little for her. He read every book he found in the library on sadness, melancholia. Haphazardly, she took her meds and saw a therapist, first one and, then, the other, not both.

To make sure she ate, Blue cooked most of her suppers; even if she was absent, he laid out her meals in hope she would return. If she prepared her own, she tended to eat too much starch or nothing at all, especially from the meals he cooked for her.

Recently, she'd tossed her old stuffed animals into their washing machine. After they dried, she brushed their nap up.

In her bedroom and its cabinet, half-glassed in and crafted by him years ago, when his kids were little, the stuffed animals stared at him from its shelves. Lying perpendicular and below to it, Lena lifted her head to thwart him, "Pop, let me sleep." Sweat matted her maroon hair. He shrugged at her wretchedness. Piglet, Winnie the Pooh, Paddington Bear, a swan, Bucky Badger (like a bear) and a green cat behind glass, and rows more of them on open shelves watched him.

Next, he escaped from his home on trial with Lena. A block from his building, Blue sank next to Harry on their wooden bench. Cyclone fencing backed it and framed it. On a triangular islet, where the highway exit met a long boulevard, a lush award-winning garden ripened beneath the dripping scarlet oak trees. Their atmosphere like Spanish moss both men knew from Florida trips. Haze also surrounded them.

* * *

As passers-by were lugging their groceries home from the supermarket past the two men, Blue probed life below their bench. "See, there're no ants in the maroon and pink peonies on the other side of the fence. They don't have ants. The grouchy gardener told me so, and I saw as fact that these big flowers housed no ants."

Blue patted his bum knee and announced, "Never liked peonies. They attract ants, except this new biotech kind.

"I read about it in Margie's latest catalogues the company still mails to her, even though she's gone."

"Antless peonies?" asked Harry. "You always find peculiarities." Lifting his arthritic leg to the right, he dropped his book.

"You got your wife and Krishnamurti. I watch ants. I've got ants. Lena studied her ant community under glass, when she was little."

"You dropped your Mutti book." The doleful mystic's face was gazing up.

"He," Harry pointed out, "takes on the world's cares. Turn Lena onto him for relief."

Blue had tried to lighten his boredom with his wife's church he was brought up in. He tried to urge Lena into it, not out, so she would fit in somewhere.

After all, Blue knew that Harry's two kids had grown up orthodox, like dittoes of their maternal grandfather. Skullcaps on their heads every day, they always greeted Blue. Why couldn't his youngest be the same way?

Soon after his wife's death, Blue recalled, by Jove, that Harry and Sally had invited Lena and him to their Seder. Blue enjoyed being invited out and not obligated to roast a leg of lamb for Easter that year. He dragged Lena along. Harry's and Sally's boys in white shirts ignored her maroon hair and managed to talk with her. Lena enjoyed Sally and her cooking for her sons and relatives.

Dressed in bright blue and her dense, light brown curls knotted up in a topknot, Sally popped away from the table. At this point in the table ceremony, she crossed the dining room to open their townhouse door to welcome Elijah. A voice outside the door sang out, "Ah, Mrs. Isaacson, could I borrow some cream," in

Norwegian Midwestern diphthongs.

On the way home, Blue speculated, "You never know, Porter might be Elijah. Or Jesus."

"Oh, Dad." Lena's voice slid in two tones.

Eventually, Lena's boyfriend met up with father and daughter as they walked home. His hair was shaved off. His beard reached his Adam's apple.

Porter also cruised along up to them. Her boyfriend, Mel, handed him a half dollar. Porter thanked him.

* * *

The next day on the bench, Blue was reading while hoping Harry would come by. He had worked as a shoe store salesman and manager until he could bend no more. Then, in retirement, he could study theosophy. Near the local state university, where Harry and Blue had lived for three decades, everyone was apt to be studying. Nobody thought Harry odd.

Blue consumed about three books a week: LeCarre, Holmes, Peukert, Smith or a second-hand *Lonesome Dove.* With his bent, arthritic and swollen knuckles, as a semi-retired cabinetmaker, he also still hammered away in his home workshop. Otherwise, he read. Hereupon Harry's arrival at their bench, Blue complained, "You and Porter make me lose my place."

"You and your Lena lose your own places." After returning to a Krishnamurti book for a few minutes, Harry paused from reading to say, "His works are the best guide for life I've ever found." Daily, Harry would sit on the bench, reading and waiting for Sally to step off the bus nearby. Meanwhile the two men "were shooting the breeze."

Usually Blue and Harry looked well pressed. Harry in his gray wash pants with his ironed work shirts and Blue in his pale brown chinos and cotton gingham shirts, worn for air in muggy weather matched well in sportiness, the more so with their baseball hats. Today, though, Blue was sweating under his light golf hat and polyester shirt.

If alone, whichever book either one read was friend until the other appeared on the cherry-stained wood bench, scratched and bleached out. At the moment, Blue was pulling a sliver from his thumb. Even Porter, "the best of the dregs in the area," relieved the tedium of a life of books, Harry said and Blue agreed. Harry clinched their link with the street man as due to "his way with words."

One day Porter told them, "All at once, I lost everything. Now I'm trying

for a studio to live in. I don't like the shelter, an old Quonset hut. Others sniff in my business or steal my stuff."

"Quonset?" Harry asked.

"After World War II," Blue said, "extra classrooms on campus got built in Quonset huts. My dad, too young for the first war and too old for the second, helped put them up for returning soldiers' classes to get back on their feet."

"Sounds Indian," Porter injected.

"Oh," Harry remembered. "Too much on our minds to notice Quonsets. Just before World War II, we got out of Germany homeless. My dad practiced law there. Here, he never recovered. But my cranky aunt came with us.

The Krauts didn't want her in the camps there. She recovered.

Blue cringed. "Your family got out?"

Harry was squinting a bit like Mutti toward Blue within a streak of sunlight through their green haze cocoon. Looking down, Blue saw his brown leather shoes were cracked and needed polishing, though Harry's sneakers were brand new, tan, what Blue would expect of a shoe salesmen and manager's shodding himself.

"My parents, my sister, my aunt," Harry said.

"Terrible. You have to watch out for those Germans," Blue declared.

"That Berlin wall should have stayed up—divide and conquer."

Just then, from the bus stop, Sally was heading up the drive. Harry jumped up to meet her.

A few minutes later, Porter filled the gap left by Harry. Breaking from panhandling, Porter observed, "Your skin's your only shelter these days. At least there's company on the street." Removing his red windbreaker in the increasing humidity and heat, he sauntered back to his concrete island.

Blue saw Porter's black skin as protective, aging better than his sun-burned, freckly neck skin. To Blue's eye, Porter also resembled a thinning six feet Santa with black hair, because of his long beard. Upon his admiring it, Matt Porter complained that in the early stage, its curls wired into his chin. "But it's better than it was ten days ago."

* * *

Christmas Eve, Blue's daughter, Lena, seeing Porter near their window, yelled down to him, "Hey, Porter." He gave her the high sign.

Her attempt at cleverness was outlandish. Blue's own arthritis made bearing his pain and her mixed-up views too much for him. He summoned the energy to admonish her. "Do you know about Porter's religion? He's a clean-cut homeless."

Outside the window, Black Santa was wearing a red cap, sweatpants, and a red/blue reversible jacket. Under his left arm was a stuffed reindeer with a Rudolph red bulb nose lit up, as if its battery was energized.

"All right," she relented. "He's a black street preppie dressed like Santa."

These days Porter, always in red, was staking out the corner incline under their side windows or else down the avenue on the island. He thumbed not for a ride but for whatever change drivers could spare.

Meanwhile, rushing down the avenue to meet O'Hennessey and Tortoricci for his weekly poker game, Blue could spare no time to chat. Nor had he loose change for Santa. Tapping away at his cabinets, when he felt like it he supplemented his pension. Otherwise penny poker absorbed his spare change. He waved to Santa Porter. The 30-year-old glad-hander was rocking between his two painful feet.

On his return from the card game, Santa Matt helped Blue carry his Christmas tree to the door of his townhouse, remodeled from old row houses for retirees. From there, Blue, his limbs aching, dragged the tree all the way inside the entrance.

A cold snap was intensifying. Frost coated

windshields unless melted with hot air. Blue could have asked Matt in out of this freezing weather. Protocol mulled over, he thanked Santa with a dollar. Porter replied, "A neighbor's a neighbor."

"Sure, sure," Blue replied. Porter's voice, while panhandling from the occasional passing car, comforted Blue at night. Urgently, Blue felt the need tofind a protective landing for the handsome homeless guy that night. He'd consulted Tortoricci and O'Hennessey. None saw the point. Blue brooded.

Porter demurred at the idea of being let into Blue's townhouse basement for the night. "I'd be trespassing. I don't trespass. I'm not the type to."

After hemming and hawing a little, Porter let Blue know there and then, "I was living with a guy. When he found out I was diseased, he threw me out.

"Out here by the red lights, when cars stop, I can raise enough jingle to pay for a cheap hotel room tonight. Besides, I'm keeping this area safe for people. The cops tell me that this corner's safer with me here."

Blue added, "My daughter and me sleep better from knowing that you, Matt, are guarding the corner." But with the wind chill at minus nine, Blue was still struggling later on over whether to invite him to sit inside his ancient Olds or his basement or the entrance to his place or the living room.

* * *

By the beginning of spring, Blue was saying to Harry about Matthew, "He's every housed person's Homeless Guy. Everyone wants to carry soup from their stove out to him, so they can feel like good folks."

"What'd you say? That he's one of those gay guys?" Harry deciphered what Blue was driving at. "You mean he got AIDS from fucking or sticking himself. How'd you find out? From the peonies?"

"I asked him. Maybe a dirty needle infected him. He told me I was the first civilian to ask if he was HIV."

"Aren't you lucky?"

* * *

One day with a glimmer of very early spring, Matthew Porter-Jones elaborated, "I came here, because my parents did. Otherwise I would have lived in the Virgin Islands."

"Oh, I came into the world," Porter commented, "a pretty happy person. My foster parents were good to me. In their house, I grew up while going to see my mother once a month. My foster parents created a pleasurable life for me. They even paneled the basement in knotty pine for me.

"The house of my foster parents went to their genetic children. My belongings remained there; the family must have sold them. I wonder if they're still there in the basement.

"The only money they could ever hand me was $97. They did say as long as they lived, I'd never need anything.

"The only caring parents I ever knew were my foster parents. Nobody located my real parents. That's what everyone told me.

"My natural father's name—Mr. Unknown. His side

was officer military. They were buried. But I don't know where. On my birth certificate, my mother's name is Olivia R.

"Just in time, I saw her, my real mother. Nine months later, she was buried. God, I miss her.

"When I entered the Navy, I was 23 with $63 in my pocket. It took me ten years from then to this past May to become homeless."

Blue clucked.

"If you ever hear me play my music, you'll remember it. Any Jamaican woman's really going to like it. I studied music. My mother used to say that Barry Manilow made a lot of money. So could I."

"I'm kind of content," Porter said to Blue. "Your wife gave me bags of cans to redeem for some change, until she passed on. Sometimes they could have been cleaner. When she died, I cried like hell. She'd just given me a rubber raincoat.

"My A.A. degree came from the community college. I should go to AA too. Maybe I'm growing to appreciate honesty. All my life I've been blessed, so I'm going back to being the person I used to be and get a job.

"After a bunch of odd jobs, I finally found a good one about five years ago with an optician, measuring eyes for glasses. When he lost his business, I lost my job. Then he started driving a limo from place to place. I met him once, when I was hitching. He offered me a ride to High Estates the last time I stayed with my foster family. He said he'd try to get me a job driving."

* * *

Blue re-entered his dim house. Mindful of the terrors of parenthood, worse than other troubles, he called out to Lena. His hand was shaking, his keys rattling as he fussed to find the light switches.

By springing lovers, not true-loves on him, Lena unnerved him more than once. Why couldn't she respect him, be discreet like the old days, as he'd been with his wife, regarding his mother or hers?

Now the silence terrified him, as he stole farther into the house. He yearned for the lovers rather than the suicidal signs. What could an old guy, not quite done in, do? He cried out, "Lena, Lena." No answer. He tore through the apartment and pounded on her door, like a drum. Lena, curling into herself, uttered, "Uh," to his shaking her.

"What are you doing? What can I do?"

* * *

Panicky the next morning, Blue almost tripped and slipped on the semi-icy sidewalk en route to the triangle island, where the avenue and side street merged. Porter also stood up from the bench, where he was holding court and announced, "Remember you paid for a copy of my birth certificate? I appreciated your help."

"Can't talk," Blue stammered. "Got a minute? My kid might be committing suicide as we stand here. Hurry, hurry!"

"You... know my state," Porter stammered. His black beard bushier and longer than before prevented his whiskers from curling back into his skin. "What life I've got left for her." He and Porter climbed the incline to

Blue's place.

Inside, together they grabbed Lena's arms, half-dragged and half-carried her to the corner, where Matt hailed a cab. Somehow, he and Blue stuffed the crumpled Lena into the cab to the ER.

After four hours of waiting, a young woman, an intake worker nearly her age, prodded Lena into her cubicle. Lena waited until another youth and another two shrinks came to shrink Lena's misery. Blue ran Porter's words over and over in his head, "Mighty, mighty."

Five days later, she left the hospital with her meds. Once in her home bedroom, she tossed Paddington Bear, Red Hen, and Bucky out the window to Porter. Having picked up a bag of groceries, Blue was watching them from the ground. Catching them nearby, Porter stashed others she threw him in his bag and carried Paddington, brown bear. "See," he called up. "Here's family for my new studio."

Catastrowtc

In the small screening room, the TV was playing the same image four times an hour. Stabbed by flying swords at 586 miles per hour, the towers fell like tents in an ancient desert storm.

A young public health investigator strolled into this low-lit monitoring room.

Hours earlier, outside her office window, she had observed the attack. Seeing the image for the first time, she screamed.

Riba, a bystander, straining to hear her words, was patting her shoulder.

An affable fellow, charged identifying persons lost within 9/11, also came to soothe the crying woman. His head sinking within his football shoulders, he interrupted the uproar to appoint Riba. "You, you look like you can oversee the phone bank for lost persons." Before his 2:00 a.m. departure, he promised to brief her. She was bewildered.

In the hush of their surroundings for public broadcasting, she was half-wondering if they were alive. Three volunteers, including Riba, were culling hospitalized patient lists for survivors, not cadavers. When a family's missing person report matched a patient, a donated teacher's bell rang out. Another person lived! Jubilee cheers arose.

Others peeked in. Regulars on the evening news,

anchors and hosts, passed by.

For hours, doctors, nurses, engineers, social workers, technicians, anyone state-licensed, had scouted for ways to help out. From a neighbor, met by chance on the train going home, Riba learned about the deployment center in mid-town. Once there, she was seated next to a Dr. Scott. Young, sturdy, brown-haired, a physician supervisor in Emergency, he treated the psychic fallout, "About twenty for panic, stomach sickness and breathing panic." One sad schizophrenic laughed at him.

"Amazing the patience here," Dr. Tom referred to the group awaiting deployment, "when people aim to give."

Arriving from another ER 100 blocks North, Dr. Collins, willow-elegant African-American, sized up the waiting persons here as "all who've done trauma work with the vulnerable...." The bullhorn interrupted her to dispatch thirty people.

Jarringly, Riba had been called first and given a choice. Go to the morgue with families of the fallen or staff the phone bank at the public broadcasting channel. She picked the phone bank.

Jingling over her late evening, early morning assignment and not knowing when she would eat again, she spotted sandwiches and grabbed two. On the way out, she met a tall, rumpled woman who introduced herself as a community department head at an international foundation. Riba told her where to find the sandwiches.

* * *

Outside, hardhats like firefighters, grave diggers, and

builders set to work pronto with heart. Singing, "Off we go, it's off to work we go," they paraded with picks and masks and stepped into the Broadway subway to Ground Zero, the area with skyscrapers being flattened.

Soft heads, state-licensed, continued to wait for vans. Reba voiced incredulity, "Stay or go home?"

"Artie," she greeted her home building superintendent like the old friend. Expecting his transfer to Ground Zero, he sipped from a bottle, one of three, discovered stacked in a pyramid next to the sandwiches. He leaned against the brick wall by the driveway. "Did we expect," she asked, "to do this?"

"God knows!" a lean, buff-skinned man named Allen replied. Below his Yankee cap, his wire glasses slipped below his keen eyes, nostrils like domino spots in a model face. At Invincibility Inc, "disaster recovery specialists" on Broadway near Wall Street, he headed security.

At 7:30 a.m. he arrived there to work. To escape by 8:50, he raced down the escalator to its atrium lobby exit. But there the density of people outside crammed him back.

The atrium security monitor, Allen continued, converted into a TV. Onscreen, a toy plane bashed the plastic skyscraper.

"On ours too," Riba agreed. Outside, smoke billowed a mile away, like bomb testing. Across the river and bridge, grit sprinkled thousands crowded along Flatbush Avenue.

Within hundreds still trapped in the Invincibility atrium though sheltered from falling debris near the epicenter, Allen told Riba, he worried about his Jane's survival nearby at 5 World Trade Center. After 7 World Trade Center crashed, as seen on the monitor, an Israeli shopkeeper gave out dust masks. An Arab shopkeeper handed out water. Awaiting this peculiar thunderstorm to pass, they stood.

"After the '93 attack on the World Trade Center," the security manager vented, "I could never coax my co-workers or managers to comply with our Invincibility plan. They joked about too much work to practice safety. What happens happens.

"Let's see if they change." The waiting volunteers huddled and conjured.

Listening in on the African American security specialist and Riba, the older side-burned, sunburned Artie, 6'6" and heavy bellied, emphasized. "THEY BETTER! Remember '93! During a job I was smoking a cigarette on Worth Street across from it when that truck bomb hit the Trade Center. Did anyone bother about it afterward?" He stubbed out his cigarette.

* * *

"About ten years later, same place, puppets were jumping out on strings. Hell, of a dumb show. Mountaineers, other climbers who climbed up trade center sides for kicks—shit, this time, those jumping down were real folks."

"So, where is your Jane?"

"She saw," Allen said, "the first tower go and rushed from her early class at Pace into the #3 train for home. I came to the volunteer center." His van arrived. He waved.

* * *

She and others from the vans reported to Dan, the instant supervisor for missing persons. In orange glow in the dark vest, he offered her one to cover her black cashmere sweater with holes in its side. Everyone here wore New York black under their orange vests.

No one trained Riba for her new post. No resume was sent. Here in TV channel headquarters, three G-men, navy vests white lettered FBI, prowled. Fearing botching her responsibility, Riba twitched.

Throughout the dark night, inquiries continued about buried souls. Callers promised and some sent by fax data on teeth fillings, scars, tattoos, jewelry to assist identifying victims.

To take charge, Riba would back up the ad hoc phone operators. When she spoke to her crew, she deepened her voice to huskiness. She strode around the phone bank room to introduce herself and called out, "Questions?" One volunteer said a caller had abandoned her cat at home, near the downed towers. Riba recommended calling the Humane Society.

Calls began to crowd out their wires, eliminating chitchat, and spread through the room. Light, Inc. in N.J. was donating transponders to sound out buried persons with cell phones under the collapse. Truth or hoax. Having consulted with Dan before his departure, she declared, "Sounds real, call headquarters."

Another volunteer called Reba over. By phone, a motel clerk was worried about a possible perpetrator of this event who'd paid for his room from a handful of 100-

dollar bills, near the Airport. Report him?

The FBI was invisible. Scratching her wavy brown head, Riba, unreal, ordered, "NYPD."

Pausing from answering calls, she murmured to callers, drawing them out. A psychoanalyst, puffy blonde-haired and flat-shoed, informed her, "I asked for the Ground Zero posting but was sent here. Sheer ageism. In my experience, I rescued people from the Battle of Britain, the Blitz during World War II." Riba felt sheepish at her own cowardice about the morgue.

* * *

Calls swirled in all night from around the country, the world, Canada, and farther: Brazil, France, Japan, India. The universe compressed into a sob.

Two hours later, an FBI agent ordered, "Bomb threat. Evacuate!" From a movie "Twin Towers", Riba waved her squadron out. "No elevator. Take the stairs." They dashed six flights down to the sidewalk.

Rumors spread. Next to the Public Broadcasting building, the Empire State Building might fall on them.

* * *

The FBI told them the Empire State scared a weary dog. The guard dog sniffed and mistook a package for a bomb.

Some volunteers, exhausted, went home. Riba and others returned upstairs to the phone bank.

Having slept through the false Empire State bomb scare, Amitia's brother awakened in the viewing room, checked on by Riba. "My building's gone."

By 8:48 a.m., witness to the first attack on the World Trade Center, he guessed hijackers were culprits. "We ran downstairs. By the 17th floor, crazy shit hit everywhere, airplane parts. Fingers, arms, legs. The sky was exploding."

His ten colleagues were missing. Only he and his manager lived.

Around the hallway corner, reassembling at the phone bank along with the tall Egyptian-American clinical psychologist, they again began answering calls.

During a respite in calls, he, two other male staffers, and Riba spoke disjointedly about Islamizing the world by knocking down skyscrapers. "I don't know," he commented, "why they did it for land. All anyone or a family needs is a small house. My wife is very upset." They thanked him for helping out.

* * *

Floor sweepers removing the litter in the wide channel hallway received gratitude and deference from volunteers. They bowed to food deliverers with turkey or beef sandwiches for meat-eaters and vegetable pasta for vegetarians.

Both opened doors for dogs to exit. One smelled a bomb, where there was none. They and everyone were still alive.

Acknowledgements

"For the Sake of Artie," *Adelaide Literary Magazine*

"Cut to Fit," *Downtown Brooklyn*

"Gyring on the Edge," *Hypertext Magazine*

"Rescue," *Downtown Brooklyn*

"Portfolio," *Artifact Nouveau*

"Adjustment," *Adelaide Literary Magazine*

"The Bench," *Saint Ann's Review*

"Catastrowtc," *Downtown Brooklyn*

About Atmosphere Press

Atmosphere Press is an independent, full-service publisher for excellent books in all genres and for all audiences. Learn more about what we do at atmospherepress.com.

We encourage you to check out some of Atmosphere's latest releases, which are available at Amazon.com and via order from your local bookstore:

House of Clocks, a novel by Fred Caron
Comfrey, Wyoming, a novel by Daphne Birkmyer
The Size of the Moon, a novel by EJ Michaels
Nate's New Age, a novel by Michael Hanson
Relatively Painless, short stories by Dylan Brody
The Tattered Black Book, a novel by Lexy Duck
All Things In Time, a novel by Sue Buyer
American Genes, a novel by Kirby Nielsen
Newer Testaments, a novel by Philip Brunetti
Hobson's Mischief, a novel by Caitlin Decatur
The Red Castle, a novel by Noah Verhoeff
The Farthing Quest, a novel by Casey Bruce
The Black Marketer's Daughter, a novel by Suman Mallick
This Side of Babylon, a novel by James Stoia
Within the Gray, a novel by Jenna Ashlyn
Where No Man Pursueth, a novel by Micheal E. Jimerson

About the Author

Survival themes derive from Jean's clinical counseling with disabled students and teaching at Columbia University. Jean studied in Italy and traveled with homestays throughout Asia and the Middle East, including Afghanistan, Iran and Vietnam. She grew up in Madison, Wisconsin with keen interest in rural and urban life. The Red Cross picked her first to help supervise the 9/11 recovery in New York City. She served as an NGO liaison to the United Nations.

The University of Wisconsin, Smith College and Sarah Lawrence College M.F.A. with Ragdale Foundation grants enabled her writing and publishing in over thirty college-related and independent periodicals. She taught and worked with preschoolers ranging to those in Ph.D. studies at the School of Social Work and School of Public Health.

Her documentary historical fiction novel *Last Gentleman in the Middle Distance* (New York and Lisbon, Portugal: Adelaide Books, 2020) was based on innumerable interviews with wartime survivors here and in Europe.

CPSIA information can be obtained
at www.ICGtesting.com
Printed in the USA
LVHW020921010821
694125LV00007B/975

9 781637 528976